THE BATTLE OF FOREVER

THE BATTLE OF FOREVER

A. E. van Vogt

NEW ENGLISH LIBRARY/TIMES MIRROR

First published in the United States by Ace Books 1971
© 1971, by A. E. van Vogt

First NEL Paperback Edition December 1973
Reprinted April 1980

NEL Books are published by
New English Library Limited from
Barnard's Inn, Holborn,
London EC1N 2JR.
Made and printed in Great Britain by
Hunt Barnard Printing Ltd.,
Aylesbury, Bucks.

45004597 8

I

MODYUN WAS feeling quite cynical by the time the speaker, having finished his talk on the new light that had been cast on man's history, asked for questions.

There were several questions of the foolish kind—people did not quite seem to know what to make of the information that had been imparted. Languidly, Modyun indicated thought and had attention.

"Are you sure you're not describing some old-style mythology?" he asked.

"We can't be sure, of course," was the cautious reply, "but we think not."

"The picture you give of our remote ancestors," Modyun persisted, "is one that considerably strains my credulity."

"Ours, also, at first," was the answer. "But the context and immensity of detail obtained provides verisimilitude."

"It would seem, then, that our ancestors fought like animals, with a sustained savagery which almost suggests that they were capable of genuine physical activity."

"That is most certainly what we have discovered."

"And like our animals, they actually walked on their own legs and did not have to be supported by artificial aids?"

"Exactly," said the speaker.

Modyun was sarcastic. "I envision somebody's delusion."

Faint, agreeing smiles registered on dozens of faces.

"I presume," Modyun continued, "they conceived and bore their own children."

"Oh, yes," was the reply. "A process of copulation impregnated the female, who thereupon gestated for a period and then delivered."

All present shuddered as this act was visualized.

"Disgusting," a woman murmured.

Another person said, "I'm afraid this is beginning to be a little hard to accept. Next thing, you'll be telling us that they ate their own food."

5

"Exactly," said the speaker. "Passed it through the alimentary canal, had a method of individual personal digestion, and passed on the excreta into a dung receiver."

There were a few more questions, but those present were now fairly alienated; the speaker, Doda, perceived this through the still-open thought-channel amplifiers by which he was connected to his "audience." Observing that Modyun was one of the still connected, Doda indicated in a private thought: "For some reason, I anticipated that you would be more interested in these discoveries than the others."

Modyun was amused. "I have a body two feet long, and a head fourteen inches in diameter. What way could I be interested in a precontrol human with eight feet of muscle and bone, capable of supporting his head himself? I perceive you have in mind my growing to that size as a scientific gesture."

"Our ancestors were more like six feet."

"Yes, but their heads were smaller, you said."

"Perhaps"—Doda's indication had a desperate overtone—"if a female were to agree to grow large, it might be an interesting experiment for you."

Modyun was instantly in a state of sardonic disbelief. "That will never happen. Our women are much too refined." He broke off, ironically, "Why not perform this experiment on yourself?"

"Because I'm the experimenter. It would take a year to grow the bodies longer, and then perhaps two years for the experiment, and then a year to become human again. Somebody must supervise."

Modyun was derisive. "Four years! When I want to ruin any reputation I have for sanity, I'll contact you."

"Don't decide against this right now," Doda pleaded. "Remember, you are the person who has said that somebody ought to go outside the barrier occasionally and see what's happening out there in the world."

"I was only joking," Modyun replied tartly.

"Still, you said it. Still—you thought it."

It was true.

Showed you, thought Modyun ruefully, that somebody was always listening with his own evaluation and purpose even to one's most casual comments . . . Unquestionably, Doda had preselected him for the experiment because he had made those remarks. Still—there were facts here . . . not to be ignored.

6

He said, abruptly thoughtful, "Surely, a careful examination of the archives and of early teaching devices, now discarded, would establish a great deal of this. Such a study would be necessary for anyone going outside . . ."

Doda was discreetly silent.

Modyun went on, "That part of it could be interesting."

He thereupon called his insect attendant, and was carried away.

Three days later Modyun was floating lazily in his private, sunlit pool. It was where he normally went to absorb the sunrays from which he extracted the energy that converted the air he breathed and the water that he absorbed through his pores into the nutrient that maintained his body in perfect perpetual health.

Well, almost perpetual. He was the third generation test-tube issue inside the barriers. Each of the previous two generations had survived about fifteen hundred years.

He floated there and gazed admiringly at his image in a sunken mirror. What a noble and handsome head, and delightful tapering body. The tiny arms and legs were partly hidden in an almost invisible harness.

Yet he could already see the hint of changes—he was several millimetres longer. For a brain as open to perception and as sensitive as his, such small transformations were clearly visible.

Doda had said that there might be a few growing pains, but these, he said, could be dealt with by properly instructing the insect scientist-aide, Eket, to inject feeling-reducing drugs into the meals he would later be taking into his body through tubes.

That, of course—Doda had pointed out apologetically—was before he actually reached the stage of eating solid foods.

Modyun shrugged aside the experimenter's concern. He had made his decision when he learned that the woman Soodleel had agreed to grow large and had agreed to associate with any male who did the same . . . There had been a slight stirring of male interest as this information was given out; for Soodleel was an extremely feminine creature who was always welcome in anybody's pool. But Doda had swiftly squelched potential competition by announcing—with Modyun's permission—that the choice was already made.

Soodleel thereupon said she was glad it was Modyun. She would follow him into size after one month.

And so here he was—years later.

7

He had been carried by Eket himself, and set down in a little grassy nook a short distance from the highway—which was beyond a brush-covered embankment out of sight.

A sound of tires on pavement came from over there. The noise stirred Modyun unexpectedly. He had to brace himself against a strong urge to jump up and down from an automatic excitement . . . a totally unanticipated body response. He kept consciously restraining his twitching muscles as he stood watching Eket depart back toward the mountains. The insect scientist was soon out of sight around an outjut of a cliff.

Modyun started up the shallow slope, still restraining himself and still astonished by what was going on inside his skin. Reaching the top, he forced a pathway through a screen of bushes. He came suddenly to the roadside.

Long ago, he had had one of his insect carriers bring him to this road. And, for a while, he had watched the traffic, the innumerable cars racing madly along. Almost every machine carried passengers: a seemingly endless number of animals of every kind. The variety of creatures had of itself roused in him a growing wonder. Because he had forgotten how many types of beast there were. All civilized now for thousands of years, and living in their man-created mechanical world.

"But where are they all going?" Modyun had finally communicated to his insect guide, a huge praying mantis originally modified for travel over the rough mountain country. The mantis had no answer except a strictly practical insect-type answer that was itself a question:

"Sir, why don't we stop a hundred or so of these cars, and ask each passenger where he is going?"

At the time Modyun had rejected that. It had seemed like a waste. But now—as he stood watching what seemed to be exactly the same rushing vehicles—he regretted that he had been too bored in that previous venture to conduct the suggested interrogation.

No boredom this time. His full-grown body felt warm with a thousand internal tuggings. Everywhere he looked, stimulation came back to him. It brought—the impulse to jiggle up and down, to twist and untwist, to move his mouth and wave his arms.

So much motion out there. The innumerable vehicles . . . The sound and sight of them reached into his ears and eyes and found his motor centers undefended.

8

The effect on him was almost like being out of control. Intolerable . . . Modyun indicated muscular inhibition. At once, all the tremblings and jerkings inside him ceased.

Calm again, he rejected an unoccupied vehicle which pulled over to him. Moments later, he signalled a car with four animals in it, and room for two more.

After it had screeched to a halt, Modyun had to run forward to climb aboard. Breathing hard, he sank with a plop into his seat. He was slightly amazed at what the exertion had produced, and noted swiftly what the responses in his body were. Increased heartbeat. Rapid lung dilation. Noisy breath inhalation and exhalation. And internal chemical changes so numerous that, after following them for a few moments, he gave up.

Interesting. New. He thought: Those drugs Doda gave me in my final growth period held me down to a sedate walk. And, of course, before that was the peaceful, gardenlike environment, stimulating only pleasant feelings.

He grew aware that the other passengers in the car were eyeing him curiously.

With that, thought of the past receded from the forefront of his mind. He eyed them back, with a small, courteous smile.

"What are you?" asked a catlike male, finally. "I don't recall seeing your species before."

The speaker bore a faint resemblance to a South American jaguar.

Modyun was about to reply that he was a man, when the import of the other's remark penetrated. Man, the ruler of the planet was—unknown.

It's true, he thought, that we do live a withdrawn existence, with our insect attendants and carriers and our household animals. And we ourselves have been uninterested in the animal and insect civilization that existed beyond the barrier.

But that that outside world had ceased to be aware of him and his fellows was another matter entirely. That was certainly not part of the original programming . . . The realization stopped Modyun from naturally uttering the truth about himself. Before he could decide what he should say, a miniscule, modified hippopotamous—a slim, eight-foot-long being who even seemed to have a little bit of a neck—who was sitting in the front seat, said, with a shrug, "He's an ape. There's lots of his type in Africa."

9

A swift objection came from the foxlike animal who sat in the rear seat beside Modyun. "I've seen lots of apes. There's a resemblance, but it's not the same."

"For God's sake," said the hippopotamous-man. "Apes are not one species like you and me. There are different breeds, and they don't look like each other."

That seemed to dispose of the argument, for the foxman stroked his jaw but said nothing more.

Well, thought Modyun tolerantly. An ape, eh? Why not?

It was a casual, of-the-moment acceptance. The failure of the programming that prevented these animal-men from recognizing him as a human being was puzzling, but it was something to inquire into. The reason for it might even make an interesting report when he returned behind the barrier.

So he settled down to play the role of ape, and to engage in a friendly discussion with a hippopotamous-man, fox-man, jaguar-man, and a darkly handsome being who presently identified himself as a grizzly bear.

All of these animal people were between seven and eight feet in height. They had had their bodies modified to a semihuman form. Each had hands, and sat erect—and of course was capable of walking erect.

In a dull way, being in a car with them was kind of interesting. Modyun leaned back in his seat, gazed out at rapidly moving countryside and felt a stirring inside him. Excitement? He dismissed that at once. Yet he analyzed that his body was having its own reactions, and he presumed that human beings had not been able in the long ago days to realize that such low-level stimulations were exactly that—purely physical and chemical.

He remembered again what the praying mantis had said that last time—about asking the motivation of a hundred animal people. So, now, he said it: "Where are you going?"

He suppressed an impulse to add the words "so fast." But the fact was that all the cars were scooting along like mechanical demons at a speed that was in excess of the original programming on such matters. Evidently the computers which handled these details had had their data altered. Upward.

By whom? Modyun wondered.

All four of his fellow passengers—they told him—had been to a training school to learn the operation of a big spaceship. And they were now going into the city of Hulee to await takeoff. He gathered that they had become buddies in camp. Their attitude towards each other was intimate, even affectionate—and, after the preliminary brief curiosity, excluded him. Which was fine with Modyun.

He felt far beyond such trivial matters. As the four discussed details of their training and talked of the forthcoming journey into space, his attention drifted. Presently, he saw that the hurtling car was entering a city. Swiftly the buildings became more numerous. They climbed hills, and were fleetingly visible beyond a distant river. Soon the city was everywhere around him. Large and small buildings glittered in the noon sun.

As he watched, he was aware that his body was again experiencing a sense of stimulation. Had he not known better he might have unknowingly accepted that he himself was excited. Have to watch out for that . . . Strong tendency of self to identify with body feelings.

The city of Hulee, he thought. Well, here I am. The first human being to come outside the barrier in about 3500 years.

There was—he had to admit it—a certain greatness about that.

II

"WHERE DO you want to go?" one of the animals asked.

It took a moment for Modyun to realize that the bear-man was addressing him. He emerged from his reverie and said he didn't know. "I'm new here. Just"—he spoke glibly—"arrived from Africa. Where do you suggest?"

They discussed the matter gravely, ignoring him. Finally, the fox-man said, and his voice held a note of surprise that they hadn't thought of it before. "Why don't we take him with us?"

And that was the decision.

"We can show him the whole gazoo," said the hippopotamous-man. "Might be kind of fun to see, for example, what kind of females he takes up with."

Modyun remembered Soodleel. "I've got my own female coming," he said.

"That's even better," said the jaguar-man. "We can watch how apes make love." There must have been an odd expression on Modyun's face, for his slightly slit eyes widened innocently. "You won't mind, will you?"

Modyun himself could see no objection, but he had an intuition that Soodleel might object. Just before his departure, she and he had gone in to observe one of his animal couples go through the sex act. Soodleel, of course, was not yet fully grown at the time, and perhaps her reaction had reflected the irritable state of her body. But she had been rather strange about the whole thing.

Smiling at the memory, he explained smoothly that female apes sometimes objected to observers.

The four males stared at him, first in astonishment, then with an almost uniform contempt. The jaguar-man said, "For God's sake, you mean to tell us you apes let your females tell you what to do."

He looked at his companions with a sly expression. "I can see we're going to have to train this fellow how to be a male." He was calm now, superior. He reached over and patted Modyun's

12

arm. "Don't worry, sir. You stick with us and we'll soon have you in a normal condition."

At this point, for the first time, the quartet of animal-men introduced themselves. The jaguar-man was Dooldn, the bear-man was Roozb, the fox-man was Narrl, and the hippopotamous-man was Ichdohz.

Having given their names, the creature-men waited expectantly. Modyun hesitated. All in a rush, memory had come of what these names meant, and how they had come about. In identifying animals, men had simply assigned each so many letters of the alphabet: five letters for animals of North America, six for South America, seven for Africa, and so on. The computers that had been programmed to name individuals had been instructed not to use all of one letter for a name. Thus there was no animal named Aaaaa or Bbbbb. But except for that the madnesses of alphabetical progression had been allowed free play. In that name sweepstake, his companions had come out rather well. Without exception their names were pronounceable.

What momentarily bothered Modyun was that men had chosen a slightly different way of naming themselves. So his name, Modyun, would instantly identify him as a human being . . . to anyone who understood the formula.

Yet his heistation was brief. He saw at once that by changing the y in Modyun to i, he could retain the pronunciation and avoid the human identification, and by adding an n, he could establish himself as being a seven letter animal from Africa. At least, he could establish it until he presented the letter combination to a computer.

Which didn't really matter. After all, it would be ridiculous to maintain this fiction of being an ape for very much longer.

His modified name was accepted without question. And so he was Moddiunn . . . for a few more hours. Or minutes.

Dooldn, the jaguar-man, thereupon informed him that he and his companions were heading for the center of the city. Dooldn said, "You understand the lodgings system here. I presums it's the same all over the world."

"Yes, I understand it," said Modyun curtly.

As he climbed out of the car a few minutes later, he realized he was nettled. Did *he* understand how these cities were operated! He who was of the race that had created the automatic cities and the automatic countryside—in short, the whole gazoo.

Nevertheless, as the car drove off, and the four animal-men walked rapidly across the wide street, it took Modyun a few moments to realize that they were heading toward a moving sidewalk.

Of course, he thought then, chiding himself.

Old memories were stirring, and the city began to look more familiar. He recalled that the residential area was structured to take care of transients in one sector, and then progressively larger permanent families, and finally there were a few luxury places reserved for human beings.

The journey on the moving sidewalk ended after a block and a half. The jaguar-man pointed up a hillside, said, "Hey, there's a whole street of unoccupieds. Let's get settled, and then go out and have something to eat."

Modyun was the last to make the four-way transition from the fast to the medium-fast to the slow, and finally to the street. His companions headed up the hill, and he followed at a slower pace, undecided. Should he continue this deception? It seemed a little futile. Nonetheless, like the others, he was presently standing before a set of buttons. He pushed the correct ones, spelling out his ape name.

Waited, then, for the door computer to open the door.

The computer refused to accept him. "You are not a properly identified person," it said.

A timeless period went by while Modyun did nothing, did not react, did not even consider what the machine had said. There was confusion inside him, a feeling he had never had before. And in a way that was a reaction, but it was brand new to him. So it was not a conscious thing, and it was not his mind being aware of a response of his body.

The fantastic thing was that the overall confusion affected his thought as well . . .

He began to come to. And his first awareness was purely observational. There in front of him was the mechanism beside the door of the apartment: the buttons he had pushed, the little triangulated metal grille below—from which the voice of the computer had spoken the incredible words.

Off to one side he could see a long line of sterile apartment buildings exactly like the one which he had selected to be his home. Well, not exactly apartments. They were all one-story high, and they spread down the entire block like a terrace. Each

14

separate unit had its little set of steps leading up to a small porch, and, he presumed—though he could not clearly make out what was beside the doors further along—that each porch had its little set of alphabetical buttons and its speaker system behind a grille.

In a way, it was a drab world that he gazed upon. Yet, how else provide housing for millions? True, if his ancestors had had the same sort of tolerant attitude toward animal-men that he had, they might well not have considered beauty, but only utility.

But since cleanliness was useful, they had provided automatic cleaning systems for each dwelling and for the city. So that the plastic wall and the plastic door and the stainless metal grille fairly shone, so clean were they. And the steps looked washed and scrubbed, and the sidewalk below showed not a speck of dirt.

He was still sort of vaguely observing the details of the world around him when it occurred to Modyun what it was that had affected him so enormously.

Rejection.

I've been rejected.

In his entire lifetime of several hundred years, nobody had ever done that to him before. The impact of it had struck a mind that had no barriers except a philosophy of the futility of things —and particularly of effort. Nothing was worth doing, really. So bodies had feelings, and minds didn't. It was the nature of a human being that he could be aware when his body had a feeling. It had been the destiny of human beings that they could choose to ignore the feelings of their bodies.

And for many moments now, he had not been able to do that. As he realized the astonishing truth of his deep disturbance— realized it again—Modyun grew aware that his body was in a state of irritation.

Consciousness of a physical feeling was like a signal. All in an instant his mind returned to its normal state: separate from the body, calm once more, but curious. He said, "What's the problem? I have a name of correct length and correct coding for an ape from Africa. What makes me unacceptable?"

"The individual of that name—Modiunn—is at present in Africa, registered as being in residence at a specific address."

The irritation was stronger. Somehow, his body seemed slightly less controllable. It took a moment for Modyun to realize what

15

it was that was so bothersome to his body. In the old days, computers could have been programmed to handle such details, but they hadn't been. No human being had ever worried about a particular animal, where he was, or even what happened to him.

So he said now in a dangerous tone, "Since when has the location of a particular animal been of concern to a computer?"

"Are you questioning my right to refuse you admission?" asked the computer.

"I," said Modyun from his height of human being, "am questioning how come you know where another Modiunn is, and I want to know who interrelated you with a computer in South Africa."

The computer said that it had been interrelated with all other computers on the planet for 3453 years, 11 hours, 27 minutes, and 10 seconds. Since it was answering, Modyun surmised that it had never been programmed against such questions as he was asking.

He parted his lips to continue his sharp inquiry, when he realized that his body was experiencing a sickish sensation. He perceived then that the elapsed time bothered some deep-feeling nerve and visceral area inside him. Exactly how long man had been behind the barrier, he did not know, after all he was third generation. But he divined from the information centers in his brain that the computers had been reprogrammed within a few years after man's withdrawal.

Who could have done it?

He made one more attempt. "You refuse to open this door for me?"

"It's impossible," was the reply. "I'm an automatic, and you don't qualify for entrance."

Modyun was unhappily reminded by the computer's statement of the limitations of a mechanical device. The problem was not the machine, but whatever—whoever—had changed the way it operated.

I'll see if I can persuade one of the others to move into a bigger place, and share it with me, he decided.

The animal-men, he now observed, had disappeared into their little houses. Modyun recalled that Roozb, the bear-man, occupied the residence to his left. So he walked there, and knocked on the door—ignoring the button system.

A pause. The sound of footsteps. The door opened, and there

16

was the handsome bear-man. The big fellow gave Modyun a welcoming smile. "Hey," he said, "you got cleaned up pretty quick. Come in. I'll be ready in a minute."

Modyun entered, half expecting the door computer to challenge him here, also. But the grille speaker was silent; the mechanism was not triggered by his and Roozb's interchange. And obviously it was not affected by the fact of his presence.

Takes the buttons, he thought, relieved.

He had intended to make his request for sharing a two-bedroom transient apartment at the door. But now that was not necessary. Exactly when he should do something, and what it ought to be, was not clear at all. But it was clear that something was not as it should be.

What had been believed was that this animal culture was a stereotype, with no surprises. Roozb's hearty invitation gave him a little more time to think about it.

I'll ask for a shared apartment . . . a little later.

III

HALF AN hour after . . .

The five of them walked to the commissary two blocks away. Inside, Modyun held back while the others eagerly grabbed plates and got into the lineup. The question in Modyun's mind was: would the food computer refuse him service? And did he want to be exposed here and now as being a human being?

What decided him to go forward was the unwillingness to believe that somebody had gone to the trouble of changing millions of these simple machines. More important, outwardly there seemed to be no sign that the slowly-built-up (over thousands of years) system of free food—with no questions asked—had been altered.

Machines automatically tilled the soil and harvested the resultant crops. For the formerly carnivorous, different types of protein substance were computer-created from the edible grains, fruits, grasses, shrubs, and trees. For the formerly herbivorous, a suitable diet was manufactured in the same total fashion. Almost everything green, yellow, or wood, had a use for some now-intelligent life-form. Almost nothing was wasted.

Too complex. Modification would have meant interfering with the entire chain of operation. Modyun took his food from containers that the automat computer allowed him to open. He used his correct name, trusting that much to his logic. After all, as he recalled it, apes still ate a variety of herbs that human beings didn't care for. And, thank you, no.

Presently, his plate scantily laden with edible food, he made his way to the table to which his companions had preceded him. Still no interference. All was well. Since they were involved in a lively discussion, Modyun sat down and began laboriously to munch and swallow. Though he had eaten many times toward the end of his period behind the barrier, the entire process remained distasteful.

He kept remembering that after he had endured the nuisance

of eating, there would come an even more degrading time. Later
. . . he would have to find a public toilet, and in the presence in
adjoining stalls of other creatures, dispose of excretory matter.

Life outside the barrier, he thought, is exactly as I perceived
it would be: a boring, tiring, irritating experience. But he was
trapped for a time in the big body, and had to fulfil its require-
ments.

He had a vision of men of old. Each individual driven, his
problems never solved, the ceaseless need to cope with his environment renewing each morning, and forcing him to continuing
action.

What thought could such a being have? Nothing.

Modyun was unhappily chewing over his food and his situation, when he realized from a chance word that his four friends
were still on the tiresome subject of their impending journey into
space.

Somebody, it seemed, had persuaded the authorities to authorize a wrong type of destination for the expedition. And they
must be counteracted, and the powers-that-be convinced of the
correct kind of stars for the supership to visit.

". . . Importance . . . necessary action . . . vital . . . decisive
for the world . . ."

The words with their implication of things that absolutely
had to be done moved through Modyun's perceptive system,
and at first he merely let them register. Finally, he took cogni-
zance of their meaning, and said with a faint smile:

"If you failed to put over your viewpoint, what would happen?"

The jaguar-being gazed at him, surprised. "Someone else
would—and in fact has put over his own plan."

"With what consequences?" asked Modyun.

"Their ideas are wrong. Ours are correct."

"But what would actually happen?" Modyun persisted.

"The expedition would go to a bunch of yellow suns like our
own. The chances of finding life on planets of suns like ours are
less than on the planets of a blue sun. That's been reasoned out."

Modyun, from his height wherein *all* such things were equally
futile, smiled again at the naive intensity of the reply. "And suppose," he asked, "the expedition found no life in either the yellow
or the blue sun systems?"

"It would be a wasted trip."

He was not reaching the creature with his perfect logic. Man had passed through such an intermediate stage himself; had believed that success consisted of one result only. Modyun shifted the emphasis of his questioning.

"On such a journey, would those who were along be comfortable?"

"Oh, yes. The ships are perfect—like great cities flying through space."

"Would those aboard eat, sleep, be entertained, associate with members of the opposite sex, have facilities for exercise and education?"

"All of those things, of course."

"Then," asked Modyun triumphantly, "what will it matter what the outcome is?"

"Because if we don't find other life, it will be a wasted journey. These interstellar ships are fast, but we've been told we're going to many planets and will be gone a long time. It's too hard on the individual if the purpose is not achieved."

It seemed to Modyun that each person aboard would have exactly the same kind of existence fail or succeed. Amused, he shifted emphasis. "All right, suppose you find intelligent life on another star system—what then?"

The jaguar-man was shaking his head. "You apes," he said, "ask the damnedest questions. For God's sake, sir, that's what it's all about, life is. Experiencing new things that mean something."

Modyun was not yet to be diverted. "Tell me," he pressed, "how will you deal with alien beings if you find them?"

"Well-l-ll—we'll have to work out a policy about that. It will depend on how they react."

"Give me an example of policy."

The creature's expression changed. He looked frustrated, as if he had had enough. "How would I know in advance!" he exploded.

While the discussion had proceeded, Modyun had noticed with a growing awareness one other implication of what had been said. Now, he asked, "You keep mentioning persuading the authorities. Who are these authorities?"

He waited, thinking: Now I'll learn who is the enemy.

"The hyena-men," was the reply.

It was, instantly, a letdown. It seemed ordinary. Not the tiger- or lion-men, Modyun thought. Not the elephant-men. Not, in

20

fact, any of what had once been the great or powerful beasts. Instead, a former scavenger had made it to the top of the power structure.

Yet it was disturbing.

Everybody had been left at an equal status. When men retreated behind the barrier, self-perpetuating computers were in charge of the cities and the countryside. The hyena-men had reasoned their way through that defensive position. Incredible— but he had no cause to doubt it.

Even so, he began to feel better. One group to talk to, to deal with, to evaluate. Suddenly, it didn't seem a serious problem.

Modyun relaxed—and for the first time really joined the conversation on the level of genuine interest. He had been reminded of something. He said, "You keep mentioning looking for other inhabited star systems. What about the Nunuli, who discovered life in our solar system? Have they been back this way? And why don't you ask them which are the inhabited systems? I'm sure they'll be glad to tell you. They were a very obliging race—."

He stopped, aware of blank faces. "Nunuli!" echoed the fox-man.

"Beings from another star! No, we never—" That was the bear.

"Where did you hear of these aliens from the stars?" asked the jaguar-man in a suspicious tone. "When was this?"

Modyun, who had momentarily forgotten that to them he was an ape, and wouldn't know any more than they, managed to say, "Where I come from is where I heard it."

Which, he thought smugly, is the absolute truth.

The four animal-men seemed to accept his statement. Evidently, what went on in faraway Africa was not that well-known to them. For a few minutes, they carried on an earnest discussion among themselves, and arrived at the conclusion that whoever had come from outer space had been allowed to leave by the inhabitants of that time, without revealing much about themselves.

It was unfortunate. Such stupidity. But it had a good side, said the bear-man. It proved that there were other races in space. "The whole gazoo out there"— The bear-man waved vaguely taking in half the horizon—"has got to be explored."

It was not exactly the right moment—their attention seemed still to be on their obsession—but Modyun's mind had gone to

21

another thought. "What did you men do before you were signed up for this trip?" he asked, curious. "What work?"

"I was a trouble shooter in the building trades," said Narrl. "You know—in these big automatic operations, things get lost like you could never believe. I found 'em."

Ichdohz, it developed, had worked on a seaweed farm by the ocean. "It still gives me a good feeling to be near water, even though it's salty," he admitted. "All those canals and ooze . . . felt good."

Roozb had been a forest ranger. "I like the mountains, and distance," he said. "That's why I think I'll like this trip. All that space."

Dooldn wouldn't tell his background. He looked slightly shamefaced. "I'm not really ashamed of it," he said, "but it was peculiar, and I'd rather not."

The refusal was momentarily a challenge to Modyun. He had a vague recollection that, in modifying the animals, man had had in mind some special ability that he detected in each species . . . What could it have been for jaguars? He could neither remember nor reason it out.

It occurred to him, belatedly, that they would want to know his occupation. He parted his lips to say that he was an electronic technician, and abruptly realized it wasn't necessary. The others were back to their tiresome subject.

The information about the Nunuli, if anything, had made them even more stirred up about their forthcoming interstellar expedition, more determined than ever—if that were possible— to insist on the right destination for their ship. As Modyun tuned in again, they were expounding a series of schemes for persuading the "authorities" to their view.

Suddenly, the fox-man leaped to his feet. "Hey!" he almost yelped in his excitement, "we'd better get over to the committee hearing."

Modyun stood up as the others did. He was slightly taken aback—though not much. Their unexpected (not really unexpected) purpose seemed to put *finis* on his vague plan to accept a room-sharing with Roozb. It hadn't occurred to him, though it should have, that there would be an afternoon meeting for them to attend.

In truth, it wasn't a genuine setback. Fact was, he might as well face up to the problem of a room. Face it squarely.

Modyun headed for the nearest door, aware of the others pressing close behind him. He was thinking: While they're off to their committee meeting, I'll confront that apartment computer. And we'll see who's boss: man, the creator, or a machine.

He walked through the door with that thought in his mind, turned to look back and discovered he was outside—alone!

IV

THE OTHERS were gone.

It was amazing.

They had been there just behind him, Ichdohz laughing throatily, Dooldn saying something in his deep, purring voice, Roozb's heavy feet stamping on the floor, and the fox-man half-barking some reply—

The words were infinitely unimportant, but the collective sounds they made had become a familiar part of his surroundings.

Modyun stopped, and looked back. There was the door through which he had come.

Not transparent, as his recollection recalled it, but—

Opaque!

He noticed as he started towards it that it had no knob, no visible latch. Three steps he took, and then his palms and fingers sought a point of entry.

Found oily smoothness. The door would not open. Behind him, from the streetside, he heard a faint noise . . . Something in his brain reacted automatically.

Modyun faced about.

The tall—over eight feet—hyena-man, who was standing only a dozen feet distant with an automatic pistol in one hand, said in an odd voice, "What happened?" Then he made a vague move with his body, a kind of wiggle, and then the pistol fell from his outstretched hand. It clattered to the pavement with a metallic sound.

And that was like a signal. The huge creature-man sank to his knees, and whispered, "I need help."

Modyun could have helped—but he didn't. He stood there, suffused with guilt.

The sensation in his brain; he realized what it had been. He had indicated gas.

Incredibly, some part of his brain had interpreted the sound behind him or, perhaps, had caught as much of the other's intent

24

as was possible in thought transference—and had interpreted *that* as threat.

What was so astonishing to him about his response was that it was aggressive.

In his entire peaceful lifetime, with its philosophy of total— but *total*—nonviolence, he had never used the attack indications of which his brain was capable.

So it's a reflex of this body, with its animallike madnesses. By God, he thought, I've got to watch that.

By the time he made that decision, the hyena-man had rolled over on his side and was lying on the concrete, doubled-up, groaning and twisting. Modyun walked over and gazed down at the tortured body sympathetically.

He saw after a moment that the pistol had been kicked several yards to one side. He went over and picked it up; broke it open and saw that it was loaded, with a bullet in the chamber.

He had no clear idea what to think about that. So he said, "Where did you get this weapon?"

No answer except groans.

Modyun persisted. "I thought guns were no longer manufactured."

This time there was a reply. "For God's sake," moaned the other, "I'm dying and you ask me silly questions."

It was not that bad. In fact, the initial feeling of strong guilt had faded from the forefront of Modyun's awareness. It was still there, but reduced in intensity by his somewhat relieved realization that it *was* gas he had indicated, and not any of several other indications.

As a result, the hyena-man was having a singularly brutal attack of stomach cramps. Possibly, there was also immensely severe heartburn, and a variety of other gassy conditions to which the bodies of animals and men were subject.

It was grim, it was painful—but he wouldn't die.

"You'll be all right in about an hour," said Modyun. "But"— he slipped the gun into the pocket of his coat—"I have a strong feeling that you intended to shoot this automatic. That makes you a potential murderer, and so I'll just take your name . . ."

Suspecting that he would not be given a willing answer, Modyun indicated automatic response. The hyena-man said, "Glydlll."

"All right, Glydlll," said Modyun, "we don't want to violate your right to your thoughts any further than that, so I won't ask

25

for any more information right now. Something is wrong in this world, and I can't believe that you are personally responsible. But I'll know how to get in touch with you when I finally make my decisions."

With that, he turned and walked off to the left where—during the swift progression of events—he had noticed an opening in a fence, which led to the front of the commissary.

As Modyun reached the street—where he had originally entered—his four animal companions came charging out of the building. As they saw him, Narrl, the fox-man, heaved a sigh of relief, and they all stopped.

For a few moments, then, their voices made a confusion of words, out of which Modyun was presently able to isolate a few bits of information—to the effect that *they* believed they had lost *him.* Modyun stared at them thoughtfully. All four radiated a kind of innocence, which made their story totally acceptable to him. Whatever had happened, they were not responsible for it.

It begins to look, he thought, as if what happened was equally simple. Quite accidentally, he had walked out of the side door at a moment when—as they now described it—they had paused and turned back to examine something. When they looked around, he was gone.

But how did the hyena-man with an automatic pistol happen to be standing outside in that backyard? The coincidence strained the imagination, but since no one knew who he was, or that he was here, it had to be exactly that: coincidence.

Modyun felt his tense body relax with that realization.

He watched the four companions hasten off to their meeting. First, they took a moving sidewalk to the vehicle street. At the gesture of one of them, one of the cars pulled over. They scrambled in, and doors shut. Moments later, the car was out in the traffic. Modyun quickly lost sight of it.

Feeling peaceful, yet slightly unhappy, he walked toward the terraced apartments. The unhappiness bothered him a little. Bodies, he thought, are really amazing. Incredibly, his body missed his four companions. It had experienced a kind of happiness in their company.

Goes to show how the minds of the original human beings got befuddled. But what was astonishing to Modyun was that the teaching machines had failed to prepare him for such pitfalls.

Whoever had programmed them had already forgotten such details. Or perhaps, knowing, had ignored them.

He was still mentally shaking his head—though he was not actually worried—over the discrepancy, when he arrived at the street where the others lived, and where he hoped to live, also. It relieved him to discover that the little house between the bear-man and the jaguar-man was still unoccupied. As a consequence of it being available, he wouldn't later have to explain why he had moved—since he wouldn't have to move.

He accordingly wasted no time, now, on further argument with a machine. What he did was one of the indication techniques by which the brain of man controlled matter. The force which was thus instantly set in motion dissolved the otherwise enduring electrical connections of this specific door-unlocking relay system.

Since he was eminently logical, he did no damage to the little switchboard by which a distant computer monitored the tiny house. Simply, he unlocked the door. And the proof of the un-locking came a moment later, very satisfyingly, when he turned the knob, and pushed. The door swung open.

He could have entered, then. But, instead, he stood where he was. And there was in him a feeling—a feeling *from* the mind to the body.

He stood there on the porch of that little housing unit, and he looked out from its modest height over a portion of the city of Hulee. And his feeling was that he was man, and these others were not as he was. Most of them had conformed, and had not changed. Man's raising of them from the animal depths where he had found them had not—for the majority—been a spring-board to a progressive development.

The biological marvels had been forced upon them. Thereafter, chains of molecules had been coded to maintain the alteration; and the coding had for thousands of years now done its exact task.

But no more and no less. Modyun visualized the vast masses of animal-men happily intermingling, going to the food auto-mats, punching in to their apartments, reporting to computers, eagerly discussing the details of anything they were programmed to do, or, as it had now developed, as they had been mobilized to do by the hyena-men.

What an astonishing happenstance that the hyena-men, of all the animal-people, were the ones who had somehow broken through the inner coding.

Yet he divined—standing there—that it was a minor breakthrough; that there was still something more in man than in any animal.

And that was the feeling in his brain.

We are the great ones, he thought.

For the first time, then, he agreed with himself that it was a good thing that he had come out from behind the barrier to evaluate What Time Had Done to Man's Planet.

With that acceptance of his presence here outside the barrier, he entered the little house where he would dwell for a while as an ape.

Until Soodleel came.

The interchange with the hyena-man with the pistol seemed irrelevant in the light of his present certainties. Briefly, the implication had been that he had become a noticed person.

But that was, of course, impossible.

So no one is looking for me, Modyun told himself. I'm an ape living as a transient in the city of Hulee.

If that pistol had been intended to kill somebody, it wasn't he it was intended to kill. That was a truth of simple logic; and therefore that possibility need be examined no further.

He accordingly ceased examining it.

And woke up in pitch darkness, aware that someone was in the room, and bending over his bed with a weapon . . .

V

HE HAD no time to consider the best reaction he could make. So he indicated solids.

Presently, he turned on the light, and got up. The hyena-man who stood rigidly poised over his bed held a knife in tightly gripped fingers. He had been caught in the act of striking down, and so his position was one of dynamic imbalance.

Modyun, who had of course never used the solids indication method on a living being before, gazed at the creature with a sense of excitement in his own body. He—the self, the thinking person—studied the intruder, naturally, with complete detachment. From what he knew about the processes that were triggered by such an indication, he analyzed that all the body potentialities for solidification had been instantly released by the hyena-man's internal chemical forces.

Modyun deduced arthritis, paralysis, stones in both kidneys, hardening of the arteries, and general calcification throughout the hyena-man's body . . . He surmised that considerable pain was involved, so he walked over and removed the knife from the hand—or rather tried to—

Not easy. The fingers seemed to be frozen around the handle. But Modyun drew it clear with an effort and a sudden tug. Then he searched the pockets of the creature-man's clothes; found some pills which, by way of intensification of his sense of smell, he identified as poisonous.

He sniffed the knife blade. Same odor. So that was the method, a double approach.

He found nothing more.

So, feeling pity for the other's agony, he indicated liquid, minimum.

The hyena-man seemed to flow down onto the bed. He lay there, giving the impression of being a soggy mass, and indeed that was almost literally what he was, for the time being.

There would be a period of internal readjustment; perhaps a

day to recover from shock to the system and reach a state of being able to move. For a while after that there would be water on the brain and too much water in every cell. But since, presumably, he was not ill, and had no natural imbalance in his system, that also would eventually rectify.

Modyun had no idea when his would-be-murderer could be questioned about his motives. He seemed to recall that the teaching machines had long ago said that it required from one to two weeks before the voice box would solidify sufficiently for purposes of speech.

All that didn't matter. What mattered was . . . No question somebody *was* looking for him.

Logic said it couldn't be, but the facts were incontrovertible. Two attempts on his life. Impossible in a world in which there was no crime. Yet it had happened.

He deduced immediately where he must go to make his first check.

And so, shortly after 3:00 A.M., fully dressed, he pushed open the front door of the twenty-four-hour commissary, and walked over to the side exit through which somehow he had—accidentally (?)—emerged onto the courtyard of the eating place to find himself confronting a gunman.

Something about that bothered him, in retrospect. A moment of confusion . . .

A thought amplifier directed me through that door, he analyzed. For instants only, it was switched on. During those moments, the amplified thought nudged him gently through that side door . . . It had seemed like his own thought. So gently, so attuned with his own purpose, that, in a noisy environment, he had failed to notice.

He presumed that simultaneously, his four animal friends had been subjected to a similar mental pressure, which guided *them* past that same door, unnoticing. But they wouldn't have been a problem, not for a moment. Animal-men had no potential awareness of such phenomena.

Convinced of his analysis, Modyun predicted to himself: The trail I am now on will lead me to a computer center, and to someone there.

And then I'll know what the problem is.

He hadn't the faintest advance inkling of what an incredible problem he would find.

Still night ... perhaps the faintest glimmer in the eastern sky ...

Modyun entered the computer center by its front entrance, and found himself in a dimly lighted world of metal panels, some of which stretched from floor to high ceiling.

There were faint sounds; as far as he could determine they were exclusively the sounds of power and power controls. Tiny clicks as one repair unit, then another, and so on either attached or detached itself from its metallic parent.

Such things meant nothing; were of no concern. It was a routine that had been going on in the same automatic fashion for millennia, and would continue, presumably, till the end of life on the planet.

What did matter was his tracer thought. He followed a single unit idea through some doors, along one corridor, and down some steps—to the unit.

Well, Modyun thought, here you are.

The machine he found himself confronting seemed to be an ordinary computer of the universal type: capable of interconnecting and interacting. Yet from it had come the guide thought that had sent him out of the side door of the food commissary.

After a moment, it was surprising to Modyun that he had been allowed to come so far without additional interference. He sensed ... resistance ... to his presence. Startling that he could get no clearer awareness, he who had such a marvellously sensitive perception.

Well, he would know soon.

He spoke to the computer, demanding an explanation. His voice made a hollow echoing sound in that room of machines. He had the distinct feeling that it was many, many centuries since *any* life noises had violated these inner spaces.

There was a distinct pause—which was itself unusual, for computers always (except now) replied at once.

Finally: "I have been instructed to inform you," said the computer, "that the Nunuli master of this planet will speak to you personally as soon as he—it—can make his—its—way to this room, which will require about a minute."

Modyun had sixty slow seconds to contemplate the meaning of those words. Since he had full mental control, he felt no reaction other than a sense of the unexpected having occurred.

The minute went by. Somewhere out of his line of sight, a door opened.

31

VI

FOR MOMENTS only, the being that walked forth from behind the array of machinery and metal paneling looked human. He was dressed in a suit that covered his body and arms. He had two legs and two arms, and the way he held them had a kind of human quality.

Modyun's second major impression was that the man was wearing a peculiar bluish green headgear, and that he had on a pair of blue-streaked gloves of a strange texture.

The moments of familiar-seemings . . . passed.

He recognized that the other was not a creature of earth. What had seemed to be colored headgear was a mass of small tentacles that rose up from a head and face that was smooth, with a glassy sheen to it.

And what looked like a suit was in fact a grayish green skin, with more blue than green in a few places. The creature wore nothing at all.

Though he had never, himself, seen a Nunuli, he recognized from what he had learned in his training periods that this was, indeed, the famous alien who had first come to earth about five thousand years before.

At least, here was one of them.

The creature had paused, and now he stood at a level with Modyun. He was about six feet tall, and seemed rather puny. The Earthman towered above him a good two feet.

Yet Modyun recognized himself as the supplicant.

"What," he asked, "is your intention?"

The arms and hands came up, and that also was a startlingly accurate imitation of a human gesture, a sort of shrug. "It's all done," said the Nunuli. "Nothing more is required. This planet is conquered."

The voice that uttered these words was soft but not effeminate. The words themselves were spoken in the universal earth language without accent. Or at least if there was an accent, it could have been a tiny regional variation.

Modyun had been evaluating the situation. "But what are your plans for myself and other human beings?" he asked.

"Nothing," was the reply. "What can you possibly do against us?"

"We have our mind control systems," said Modyun.

"How many of you are there?"

"About a thousand," Modyun admitted reluctantly. For a moment—for just a moment—he was impressed by the smallness of the number.

"When we first came here," said the Nunuli, "there were nearly four billion human beings. *That* could have been dangerous. But now, I tell you we're quite willing to let those thousand do anything they please . . . including resisting us. But why should they bother us if we don't bother them?"

Modyun considered that with—he realized—a feeling of relief in his body. A tension had been building up in his body muscles and nerves, and the feedback from that to his mind had been rather overpowering.

He said finally, "But why did you conquer us at all? What are you going to do with a planetful of such a variety of so many intelligent life-forms?"

"What's to be done with this planet," said the Nunuli in a formal tone, "has not been decided. A decision will be made at a future meeting of the committee." The creature made the familiar shrugging gesture, spreading his hands and arms, and said, "It's sometimes difficult to get these matters onto the committee's agenda."

"But why did you conquer us in the first place?" persisted Modyun.

The Nunuli reverted to his formal tone: "Our instructions were to conquer the ruling group—after which a decision would be rendered as to the disposition of the planet. Our method of conquest on earth was to offer human beings improvement of their then bodies and brains. Your ancestors were so impressed by the abilities which were thus released, that they failed to notice that among the tendencies thus stimulated was an overwhelming impulse to retreat into a philosophical existence.

"As the process continued, human beings soon were willing to leave their civilization to be run by animals and insects. Later, when we wanted an animal group to represent us, we chose the hyena-men. Naturally, not understanding the situation

3

33

clearly, they don't represent us very well. So you were inconvenienced—"

Modyun presumed that the reference was to the two attempts on his life. It seemed an unsatisfactory explanation, but he offered no comment.

"That," the Nunuli was saying, "won't happen again—unless you prove difficult."

Modyun, visualizing in a sweeping appraisal all that had been said, drew a deep breath, and said, "It scarcely seems like a conquest."

"Man has virtually disappeared. That's conquest."

It was a difficult idea for Modyun to appreciate. The cutting down of a species to a representative thousand seemed rather sensible to him, one which could well be followed by the Nunuli and the huge numbers of animals and insects that swarmed all over Earth.

He said as much.

The Nunuli rejected the concept. "Our instructions are to conquer the universe, and to breed exactly the quantity of subordinate peoples progressively needed to accomplish this goal."

"But why?"

"That is for the committee to determine," was the cold reply.

A vague picture of the hierarchical structure of the invaders was beginning to form in Modyun's mind. He said, "This committee, do you communicate with its members?"

"No, they communicate with us. We receive instructions."

"They don't live among you then?"

"Oh—no!" The Nunuli sounded shocked. "They live behind a barrier, and no one goes there. But no one."

"Are they like you? In shape, I mean."

"Of course not. That would be slightly ridiculous." The Nunuli was suddenly indignant. "The members of the committee are a special race."

"How many of them are there?"

"Oh, about a thousand," was the reply.

"I see," said Modyun.

It was evident from the words spoken by the creature that *it* did not see. The words were, "A committee should not be any larger. It would become too unwieldy."

"Of course," said Modyun hastily.

He added, after a moment, "I observe that our animal people

are being sent out into space to other worlds. Apparently, you are using them as a part of your invasion force."

"Of course. They act as auxiliary forces in our conquest system."

"Then the hearings as to where the big ship—which is now being readied for flight—will go, are just a camouflage?"

"On Earth," said the Nunuli, "we maintain the image of the democracy originally set up by man. Thus we have hearings and the appearance of freedom of choice by the majority. But the fact is, the planets to be conquered have already been selected."

"But at present," said Modyun, "you have no plans to deal with the peoples now living on Earth . . . in any final manner?"

"Until the committee," said the Nunuli, "renders a decision in connection with what shall be done with Earth. What the inhabitants do meanwhile is immaterial—now that Earth is a conquered planet."

The being concluded, "I analyze that it may be inconvenient for us to have you around as the time for takeoff nears. So I recommend that you return behind the barrier."

Modyun said, "It seems to me that so long as I maintain my guise of being an ape, I am no problem to you if I remain around."

"Sooner or later," was the reply, "someone will recognize you, and that will create a complication. So, leave the city . . . is my advice."

Modyun persisted. "Although, as you know, we humans do not use aggressive abilities, I have the impression that if I were so minded, I could exterminate all the Nunuli on this planet. Am I wrong?"

"Apparently," was the irritable reply, "we're going to have to prove to you that the smallness of your present numbers literally renders you impotent. So on that note, I think this conversation should end. You may go out of this building the way you came in."

So here he was, the morning after.

As he awakened, Modyun reflected that it didn't feel any different to be living on a conquered Earth than before he knew.

It wasn't as if the four billion men and women who had gradually bowed out of life—always for the extremely good reason that living was too much trouble. It wasn't that anybody had massacred them. Or worse—presumably—that they were still to be exterminated.

The job was done, and it had been done quietly by the individual himself. Could such a fate be attributed to premeditated conquest?

The question belonged in philosophy.

VII

The thought completed.

He abandoned further consideration of it. And got out of bed.

As he finished dressing, he heard footsteps on his little porch. He opened the door.

His four animal friends stood there, somewhat differently dressed from the day before. Now, each of the creature-men wore not only slacks, but a matching coat. Under the coat was a white shirt with a high collar. And fastened about the collar, and drooping down, was a bright-colored scarf. Even their feet were differently arrayed. The previous day they had worn a kind of nondescript slipper. But this morning they had on gleaming black footwear.

Modyun surveyed the four in mild astonishment. Before he could speak, the bear-man said in his genial voice, "Thought you might like to go along with us for breakfast."

A deep-down body warmth welcomed the invitation. And Modyun himself did not actually hesitate. Truth was he had nothing to do until Soodleel came out of the barrier. It had occured to him that it might be vaguely interesting to make a tour of the planet; the precisionists would expect him to document his account when he rejoined the human race. But the tour could wait. At least, he smiled, until after breakfast.

He walked out onto the porch. Turned. Closed the door behind him. Faced forward again. And this time shook hands with each animal-man. Narrl last. Narrl said, "We got lots of time. Committee meeting doesn't resume until eleven."

It was another bright day. As they walked along, Modyun breathed deeply of the air and found it pure and fresh, still. So that was not being, and had not been, interfered with. At ease, he said, "How did you make out at yesterday's hearing?"

Four disgusted groans answered him. "Those hifalutin', hyena-men!" complained Dooldn. The others expressed similar sentiments, and what presently emerged from their critical reaction

37

was that they had not been allowed to testify because they were not properly dressed. And so they had sat in the audience and listened in frustration while inept witnesses for their point of view were made fools of by the commission.

"We're sure gonna put a stop to that today," muttered Dooldn in his purring voice. The slant of his eyes and the hint of jaguar rage in a brightening pink spot on each of his cheeks, lent his words a certain ferocity.

Remembering what the Nunuli had said—that the destination of the big ship was already selected—Modyun felt sorry for his companions. Whereupon, his body had an impulse. "Why don't I go with you?" he volunteered. "I'd like to observe some of these hyena-men myself. I won't testify. Just watch."

That was true. He really would like to look them over.

The four animal-men were delighted. "We can have you tell them about Nunuli," said Ichdozh. "But he'll have to get some better clothes," grunted Roozb. "Get real dressed up like we are." Modyun repeated, "I don't plan to testify."

By the time they had breakfast, and had borrowed a suit for him, time had telescoped the morning. Modyun hurried with the others to the street where the cars were racing along. Almost at once, a vehicle pulled over and picked them up.

Their destination was a tall building in the center of the city. An elevator carried them to an upper floor. Once in the corridor, his companions assumed an attitude of subdued respect, and soon were whispering their intent to an eight foot hyena-man, who stood before the closed double-door entrance to what was evidently a conference room. The creature-man nodded, admonished silence, and very gingerly opened the door just wide enough so that they could enter in single file.

Modyun sat in the rear of the hearing room, and gazed out over a large number of strange heads. There were even a few of the small breeds of insects—no carriers, of course. These also (it developed) were there to testify and to urge their point of view. Modyun did not listen to the testimony itself, so he was unaware of what they wanted.

His attention was on the commission: hyena-men, everyone. It was amazing. He felt a strong desire to get closer to them. He observed that the people who got the closest were those who testified, and so it occurred to him that he might, in fact, find out most about the hyena-men if he were to challenge the

38

right of the committee to sit in judgment on the matter. So, why not?

Accordingly, as Narrl—a little later—completed his impassioned pleas, and was dismissed, Modyun beckoned him to come over. And to him he whispered that he had changed his mind and would like to have his name placed on the list of testifiers.

The fox-man, who had bent down during the request, straightened to his height of seven and three-quarters feet and said aloud in surprise, "Of course, we put in your name right at the start. We want you to tell 'em about the Nunuli."

His voice was momentarily a disturbingly loud sound, and the clerk of the committee rapped sharply for order and silence. But in due course there was Modyun in the witness chair. Whereupon, one of the committee members addressed him politely, saying, "It says here that you're an ape. I've seen apes, and you don't quite look like any ape that's come my way."

"There are many breeds of apes," Modyun paraphrased the argument given in the car by one of his animal companions.

"Which breed are you?" his questioner persisted.

Modyun dismissed the question from his attention. He was interested in this closer view of the ruling animals of earth. The hyena-men he had seen before, outside the commissary and in his bedroom the day before, had not, in their sick condition, been suitable subjects for study.

He suspected that it might be equally difficult to determine from a human being with severe stomach cramps or arthritis the reasoning power of *that* breed.

So now he gazed intently.

And clearly there was a difference . . . at once apparent.

Yet the outward appearance was of ordinary, modified animals. The original hyena head shape was there, but barely . . . exactly as were the other animals and their original shapes. Like the others, the hyena-man's countenance was almost human, so thorough had been the biological manipulation into a manlike shape.

The difference was subtle, but definite. Modyun detected a feeling of superiority, an attitude of acceptance of themselves as better. Their logic: they ran the planet, therefore, they were superior.

The question in his mind was: did they know that they were the agents of an alien race? Was theirs a conscious association

39

with the Nunuli? The answer to that was not detectable in the hyena-men on the hearing board.

As this chain of perceiving completed its swift course in Modyun's brain, he decided to make a direct challenge of the status quo.

So he said, "Would you please quote to me the human directive that permits a hyena-man to consider such matters as this?"

There was a stir in the audience. Feet shuffled. Even a sense of heavier breathing, and a murmur.

Down came the gavel, rapping for silence. The committee member, who had already spoken, raised his eyebrows and tilted his head back; then he recovered and said, "Your question is not one that this committee can adjudicate. We operate under a directive of a government department, and our purposes are entirely within that frame. Does that answer you?"

Modyun had to admit silently to himself that it did. He had neglected to find out who he was challenging, and so he found himself confronting a subordinate organization. It was one of those—not endless, but circuitous—chains of command—like talking to a computer instead of the person who had programmed it: pretty useless.

They're all gentlemen, he thought.

It really looked very civilized and orderly. He realized he was not that opposed to anything that had achieved their level of culture.

"Under the circumstances," he announced to the committee, "I have no further testimony to give at present."

As he rose to his feet, and stepped down from the dais, the jaguar-man yelled from the audience, "Hey, what about the Nunuli?"

Evidently, that was too much for the hyena-men. The gavel pounded furiously. Hyena-men in uniform came rushing in. In a few minutes, the hearing room was cleared of its audience, and a notice read out in the corridor that the hearing would resume that afternoon at three o'clock.

Modyun, walking along toward the elevators with his friends, rounded a corner—and grew aware that a score or so hyena-men in uniform blocked the corridor a hundred feet ahead. As the spectators and witnesses, who had attended the hearing, came to this living barrier, each individual was stopped and spoken to. In every case that Modyun observed, the reply seemed to be satisfactory; for the person was then allowed to proceed along a narrow pathway made for him through two rows of uniformed hyena-men.

The little group of five had to wait in a lineup for their turn. Narrl, who was in front, presently reported back, "They're asking each person his name. As soon as he gives it, he's let through."

The hyena-man, who did the questioning, was a stern-faced individual with a document in one hand. After Modyun gave the ape version of his name, the officer glanced down at this document, and then said in a formal tone, "Will you spell that?"

Patiently Modyun did so. Once more the creature-man examined the paper he held. "This is for you," he said. He held the document out to Modyun. The human being accepted it, but he said, surprised, "For me? What is it?"

"A summons."

"What's a summons?" asked Modyun, interested.

The being was irritated. "Read it," he said. "That'll tell you what it is." He made a gesture toward the other uniformed hyena-man. The entire group stiffened. "Face right! March!" ordered the commander. The sound of their footsteps faded rapidly.

As Modyun stood there beside Roozb, his other three friends stared at him. "What was all that?" asked Roozb. "What did he give you?"

"A summons," Modyun replied.

"A what?"

Modyun handed it to the bear-man. The big fellow peered down at the folded paper, and then slowly read aloud the words on the top fold: "*State versus Modiunn.*" He looked up. "Hey," he said, "that's you all right. But who's this guy, State?"

Modyun could not suppress a smile. "The state is the government." He paused. His smile faded, as he considered the meaning of his own words. Finally, he said, "Presumably, that refers to the usurping hyena-men."

He saw that the faintly pink face of Dooldn was twisted into a frown. "That was a good point you made, Modiunn, at the hearing. How come hyena-men have the right to decide where this ship is going?" He was scowling now. The thick muscles of his jaw rippled peculiarly. He clamped his teeth together with an almost metallic click. He finished, "I never thought of that before."

41

"Yeah," said Roozb, "That was a good point. Why, hell," he said, "you and I"—he glanced at the jaguar-man—"could take on a dozen hyena-men all by our lonesome. So where do they come off telling us what to do?"

Modyun looked quickly from one to the other of the two powerful animal-men. Both men's faces were flushed; and it was obvious that some wellspring of emotion had been stirred inside them. The human being thought: The savagery is really not too far below the surface. He was surprised, but—

It decided him. Better take care what he said in the future. Obviously, it would do no good to rouse these creature-men because they could only get into trouble.

Aloud, he said, "Calm down, fellows. Let's not get ourselves excited. Whatever this is, is not that important."

A moment longer, the tableau held. Then the high color began to fade from their faces. Dooldn reached out and took hold of the document in Roozb's hand. "Let's take a look at this," he said.

"Wait," objected the bear-man. But his reaction was too slow. His friend had the summons away from him, and was unfolding it. The jaguar-man stared down at the first words on the inside, and he seemed struck speechless for a few moments by what he saw there. Then he read aloud, "Criminal Summons."

"Criminal?" echoed Narrl.

All four animal-men, almost as one, drew away from Modyun. They stood there, then, and stared at him.

Their faces showed puzzlement now. Briefly, the overall aura of innocence was missing from them.

Modyun said, "How can I be a criminal in a world where there is no crime?"

"Yeah," said Roozb. "He's right. What could he have done?"

"Well, I don't know . . ." It was the fox-man, and he sounded doubtful. "If the hyena-men say he's a criminal, I suppose that's got to be the way it is." He broke off. "It's all very well for us to argue about how they got to be the government. But the fact is that's what they are."

Modyun said to Dooldn, "You've got the written charge there. What does it say?"

"Say, yeah," said Roozb, "read it."

The jaguar-man thereupon again held the sheet up to the ceiling light, and said in his soft, deep voice, "The charge is—yeah—

here it is—damaging a computer outlet, falsely gaining entrance to a transient residence . . ." He blinked. "Hey, that doesn't sound like a serious offense." Again, he glanced down at the summons. "It says here you've got to appear before a magistrate next—uh—Tuesday . . . Until then—listen to this—all honest citizens are suborned from associating with the accused. That's us, honest citizens. So"—he shook his head at Modyun—"you'll just have to be a loner until next Tuesday."

Hastily he folded the summons and handed it to Modyun. All sign of his brief rebellion of a few minutes before was gone. He said, "Well, fellows, we'd better get out of here." To Modyun, he said, "See you next Tuesday, buddy."

He walked off, followed by Narrl, who waved a casual good-bye. Roozb and Ichdohz were hesitant. The bear-man growled uncertainly, "You can't just walk away from a friend in distress."

Modyun had reaffirmed his decision not to involve these people in his affairs. "Only until next Tuesday," he urged. "See you then."

The words seemed to be the reassurance that the bear-man and the hippopotamous-man needed. They were visibly relieved and shook hands with him almost gratefully. Then they hurriedly departed after their two companions.

By the time Modyun, going in the same direction, arrived at the elevator shaft, there was no sign of the four. In fact, there was no one around at all. When the next elevator arrived, Modyun saw that it was empty. Which was also surprising. Nonetheless, he was on the point of entering when the impact of the total absence of people from an area that five minutes before had swarmed with them, brought a cautioning thought.

Wel-l-l-ll, I'd better walk down, he decided. Have to remember the Nunuli is a cunning type.

It would be unfortunate if that particular elevator were to get stuck on the way down, with him in it. To escape, he might have to break a few more laws . . . As he headed down the first flight, it occured to Modyun that he was making a complicated response to a simple situation.

I suppose, he sighed, on starting down the second flight of thirty-three, this is what people had to think of in the long ago days when there was competition and scheming, and all that.

Going down the third flight, he was conscious of a distinct aversion to this life outside the barrier. Perhaps he ought to do what the Nunuli wanted: go back there and forget all this madness.

But, he realized sadly while descending the fourth flight, "I promised Doda. And, besides, in a few weeks Soodleel will be coming."

So there was nothing he could do except walk down thirty more stories.

Which he did.

Yet by the time he arrived in the lobby, he had come to a decision.

Accordingly, he indicated awareness.

VIII

PEACE PERVADED the all . . . with here and there disturbance.

Modyun sensed his oneness with the entire near universe—except for the areas of disturbance: the interposing, interacting, aggressing energy of—violence, it was called. Or perhaps, violent intent. Whorls, and chains, and darknesses, and glittering strands, and streams of hard, bright silveryness vibrating in the otherwise peaceful vastness around him.

He perceived that the animal-people were peaceful dupes. There were so many of them that their overall goodwill filled the void.

The hyena-men produced a mix in his perception of the surrounding grid. The great majority were unknowing dupes. The shiningness, tangled with darkness strands, showed no awareness of how they had become the power group. But—no mistake about it—they accepted their role. And so from them there was a steady effluvium of mild aggression. Their continuing purpose created . . . tautness; yes, a rigidity. But nothing really serious.

The hyena-men leaders, however, were a different coloration. They *knew*. The knowledge elated them. Around those aware individuals there were clouds of the peculiar self-admiration particles and emanations. Theirs was the glee of the totally secure. A security that derived from a consciousness that the Nunuli were all-powerful, and that accordingly those through whom the Nunuli ruled, were absolutely unassailable.

. . . Pride of position intertwined with a timeless euphoria—the fabric of space was twisted into numerous special configurations. There were well over a thousand, too many to count; an entire hyena-man upper class. And around each individual there was shaped an aggressing pattern . . .

Yet the real disturbance came from the single Nunuli. Around him was a huge formless black condition. An impenetrable veil covered that being.

The blackness drew power from a nearby source. But that

source had no obvious location. The power that came from it was a little startling even to Modyun.

Hey, that's Ylem, the basic stuff.

Say, I have made a key discovery about the enemy.

The awareness poised, with that thought, It rejected the concept of enemy because . . . are there any enemies, really?

The whole inner meaning of the peace philosophy said no. There are no enemies. There are only people who, by their actions, draw to themselves a response.

This response, which they themselves have evoked, they then label as having come from an enemy.

But the true enemy is in the impulse in the—however momentary—disturbance, which causes them to do the thing that brings the response.

No response, no enemy.

So, decided Modyun, I shall return to my little apartment, and stay there creating no problems, evoking no responses, until next Tuesday . . . when I go to court. Which is the peaceful reaction to the summons that has been handed me.

And that was exactly what he did—except for going out to eat.

IX

THERE WAS a man at the door wearing a name card that read: SUMMONS CLERK. This hyena-man examined Modyun's summons, and then said simply, "Enter, sir."

Modyun entered the big room, and looked around, puzzled. Directly in front of him was a long desk. Behind it, beyond little transparent wickets, were about a dozen hyena-women. In front of each of these wickets was a lineup of animal people. The line-ups ranged in number from six to twenty.

No sign of a courtroom. He went back out into the corridor, and glanced along it at the other doors. Then walked slowly to the nearer ones. His thought, that perhaps the wrong number had been printed on the summons, faded. There was still no sign of a courtroom.

He walked slowly back to the big chamber, showed his summons again to the "Summons clerk"—who seemed to have forgotten him—and was admitted once more. This time when he got inside, he approached a uniformed hyena-man, who stood off to one side. On *his* nameplate were the words: COURT CLERK. Once again, the summons was the acceptable communication. The "clerk" glanced at it, and said indifferently, "Window eight."

Modyun walked over and took up a rear position. It was the shortest line, consisting now of five persons. Modyun was six.

He had barely joined the lineup—and just barely had had time to notice that the first in line person was a tiger-man—when that individual was handed a slip of paper through the wicket. The tiger-man glared at it. Then he bent down and said something through the opening. Modyun did not hear what the words were, but there was no mistaking the emotion that prompted them: rage. The hyena-woman's answer came surprisingly distinct. She said courteously, "I'm sorry, I don't make the laws."

The tiger-man straightened slowly. Then he stood scowling, for at least ten seconds. Finally, jaws drawn into a muscular looking knot, he walked abruptly off toward the door.

47

The rat-man directly in front of Modyun shook his head and whispered, "Boy, that sure must have been a heavy sentence."

Modyun said, "What was the offense?"

The other man shook his head. "It's on his summons." He added, "Probably beat up on somebody. Those are the big penalties."

"Hmm," said Modyun. He was curious. "What's your offense?"

The rat-man hesitated. Then: "Stealing."

"Stealing! In a world where everything is free." He was genuinely surprised, and it was only after he had spoken involuntarily that it occurred to Modyun that his words might be offensive.

And in fact the rat-man's first response was, "For God's sake, things aren't that great." Having said that, he relaxed, and seemed to accept at least a part of the implication of Modyun's astonishment. He continued in an easier tone, "It is kind've hard to imagine, but I got to noticing something. You and I—" suddenly, he was indignant—"can take those general cars on the main roads. If we want to go up a side street, we've got to get off the mainline cars and walk over to a moving sidewalk, or just plain walk."

"What's wrong with that?" Modyun asked. He spoke in a neutral tone. "When those details were figured out, it seemed like a very fair method. Nobody ever actually has to walk more than a hundred yards."

The thin face in front of him with its hint of rat shape, twisted into a knowing smile. "When I noticed that hyena-man officials have special cars that drive right up those side streets—well, I figured I was just as entitled as anybody. So I took one and drove it home. And here I am."

As he spoke, they moved forward in the lineup. When that was done, and Modyun had taken time to glance at the face of the person who had been sentenced and was now departing—it was an expressionless countenance, reminiscent of a crocodile, or at least of a reptile of some kind, and told him nothing—he returned his attention to the rat-man, and said, "How did they catch you?"

"They're connected, these private cars," was the disgusted reply, "with a special computer. The computer sent a hyena-man patrol after me. So I was handed my summons to report for trial today, and here I am."

48

"Doesn't seem like much of a trial," commented Modyun, as the third man in the lineup accepted the card with *his* sentence presumably printed on it, glanced at it, showed his rabbit teeth in dismay, and bounced off toward the door.

The meaning of Modyun's words didn't seem to sink into the rat-man's awareness. "Oh, well," he said, "a court is a court."

It didn't look like a court to Modyun.

"You and I"—the rat-man shurrgged—"just had tough luck, and so here we are in court."

The fourth man was turning away from the wicket. The rat-man said hastily, "I'd better face forward. You have to show respect in your manner, or else you may be considered to be in contempt of court."

"What's your name?" Modyun asked.

It was Bunlt, and he was a permanent resident of Hulee, with a wife, and three offspring. Bunlt wanted to know why Modyun was interested in him.

"In a world," said Modyun, "that's perfect except for people having to walk a hundred yards, you steal. I'd like to learn what your philosophy is—"

Bunlt did not reply. He was being handed his sentence. He glanced at it, and his face acquired a taut, unbelieving expression. He walked away looking dazed. Modyun would have liked to go after him, but it was his turn. And so he pushed his own summons under the grille, and watched with considerable interest as the hyena-woman punched the numbers from it onto a machine to her right. The slip of paper that rolled out had some of the stiff appearance of a card.

Modyun accepted the little slip of paper with considerable interest, and read: "Penalty: Twenty days confinement to your quarters. You may go out to eat three times a day, taking not more than one hour for each meal."

He was enthralled. He bent down, and said to the woman, "This seems a little illogical. My offense is occupying quarters illegally. Now, I'm confined to those same quarters, and apparently it will no longer be illegal for me to be there. Is there somebody I can discuss this with?"

"Please step out of line. Ask the clerk for any information you want."

Modyun, who during his own "sentencing" had sort of out of the corner of his eye watched Bunlt disappear past the Summons

Clerk, and had delayed only long enough to ask his brief question, straightened and strode hastily to the same exit himself. Arriving in the corridor, he scanned the people near and far, looking for Bunlt.

Saw him not.

Well, he must have really made a run, and forgotten my request completely. Too bad.

Shaking his head, as he had seen Roozb do on several occasions, Modyun turned to go back into the courtroom. His passage through the door was barred by the Summons Clerk.

"Have to have a summons to get into the courtroom, sir," the hyena-man said politely.

Modyun explained what had happened, and displayed his sentence slip. The door guard, for that was what he was now turning out to be, shook *his* head. "Sorry, sir, I have no instructions about anyone coming in here without a summons."

"Well-ll," said the human being. He took a step backward. And he stared at the problem creature blocking his passage, and thought: After all, the whole court business is a travesty. It would be ridiculous to ask about the irrationality of one aspect when the entire procedure was an injustice.

Still, a few details bothered him.

Aloud, he said, "Could you tell me what kind of sentences are handed out here? For example, that rat-man who departed just ahead of me. What kind of penalty would be meted out for what he did? Stealing a car."

The door guard drew himself up to his full height. "Sir," he said, "those of us who have the inner power to rule have also the compassion whereby we long ago decreed that a court penalty is the privileged information of the sentenced person."

Modyun protested, "I can't see how secrecy is of any value to a person who has been wrongfully penalized."

The guard was calm. "Please step aside. You're interfering with court business."

It was true that another person with a summons had come up at that moment. Modyun backed away, stood undecided, then walked off towards the elevators.

He had had his day in court, and it was now time to begin serving his "sentence"—at least until Soodleel arrived.

X

As THE car pulled to a screeching halt, Modyun saw the woman standing beside a clump of brush, partly out of sight. His was a quick glance only. Because he was late, and correspondingly guilty, he leaped from the vehicle, and ran towards her. He was unhappy now with the fine-timing job he had tried to do, so that he would not be too long away from his apartment-prison.

Even though he had skipped a meal to give himself extra time, he analyzed that he was already overdue. So—quick. Get her into a car, and head for the city.

As he had that thought, he climbed the small rise up to the bushes where she was—and from that height saw Eket. The insect-scientist was about a hundred and fifty meters up the valley, and was unmistakably in the act of going back behind the barrier.

The sight reminded Modyun. He stopped, and indicated thought on one of the insect bands. First, he greeted the insect, and accepted a courteous greeting in return. Then he gave his message for the other human beings.

In his mental report, he described briefly what he had found. The changes in computer programming. The new status of the hyena-men. The Nunuli conquest of Earth on behalf of a distant committee.

What he said was merely intended as information. Obviously, interest in such details among real human beings would be minor. Perhaps, a few individuals would even be titillated. Possibly, Doda would be gratified and feel justified in his having undertaken his much-criticized experiment. (A few males were particularly critical of the fact that he had involved Soodleël.) Nevertheless, it was doubtful if anyone else would be motivated to become a self-supporting body, with all those degrading needs.

The concluding words of Modyun's communication took into account such potential reaction of those who remained behind the barrier.

Through Eket, he transmitted: "Since Soodleel and I are condemned to another three years of enduring the purgatory of full-body existence—two of those years out here—I would suggest that you leave the solution, and all further consideration, of the above data and reality to us."

That completed the message.

Though his communication was brief in point of time, Modyun was aware of the woman walking out of his sight. For just a moment, he hesitated. And looked out over the hazy valley to where the insect carrier was rapidly disappearing.

What bothered him for that moment was the feeling that he had transmitted a falsehood. The truth was, he was not dealing with the situation, and he doubted if Soodleel had any intention of solving it either.

The feeling passed. Because—what did it matter? What could the Nunuli do against human beings? Nothing . . . it seemed. With that thought, he started around the clump of brush. Rounded it. And stopped. And stared.

For God's sake, he thought.

Soodleel was standing beside the highway, watching the ceaseless traffic. She was only about thirty metres from him, and at first she showed no awareness of him. Modyun started forward—and she turned to face him. Instantly, what had already astounded him, intensified.

Her aliveness! It was absolutely startling. She was smiling as she looked at him. It was an electrifyingly beautiful smile. There she stood, somewhat awkwardly dressed in a pair of trousers and a shirt. But her golden hair fell down to her shoulders. Her blue eyes were so bright that they almost seemed to shine with a light of their own. Her lips were slightly parted, and the overall effect was of a brilliant-personality on the verge of—what?

Modyun had no idea. He had never looked at a woman who was human and full grown. What made her appearance so unexpected was that, a few weeks ago—when he had last seen her—she had been measurably smaller in size. And there had been about her a kind of dullness, which Doda had attributed to the extremely rapid cell growth. And of course to drugs.

All that was gone.

Suddenly, here she was radiant with health. Her whole body and face projected a vibrance. And it went on and on, never ceasing for a moment. This stunning apparition said in a golden-throated voice, "Eket let me overperceive your message to the others."

The woman added, "So that's the problem."

Modyun discovered his own voice at this point. "That's a part." He went on hastily, "Let's get into a car, and I'll tell you the rest."

He was anxious now. He was really overdue in his apartment, and the sooner they were en route the better that situation would be.

Soodleel offered no objection to his suggestion. Modyun, accordingly, signalled an unoccupied vehicle. They climbed in, and he began his tale. How he had been mistaken for an ape. Of how he had permitted the misidentification out of curiosity. And of the consequent confinement to his apartment as a penalty for obtaining living quarters under a false name.

When Modyun had finished his summary, Soodleel said, "Your sentence is for twenty days?"

"Yes."

"And you have now served eighteen?"

"Yes." A puzzled tone—because she seemed purposeful.

"Do you think there is anything significant to it being exactly twenty days?" asked the woman.

"How do you mean?"

"Well, they needed twenty days to accomplish something in connection with you, and wanted you inactive during that time?"

It was a totally new thought. But Modyun recovered swiftly from its implications. He said, "What can they do in three weeks that they can't in three days?" He broke off, finished more simply, "I assumed I received a sentence to fit the crime."

"Then you believe that many animals give a false identity?"

It occurred to Modyun after a pregnant pause that he didn't believe anything of the kind, and that in fact he doubted if anyone had ever been sentenced for that "crime" before.

He said slowly, "It does seem odd, but the fact is, what can they do? What can their committee do?"

Soodleel's even features had been twisted into the expression of someone trying to grasp a difficult concept. With his words, she smiled that brilliant smile. And, just like that, she was beautifully intense again. "That is true," she agreed. "So there really is no problem. I was curious."

Her dismissal of the matter, after she had brought up such a good point, did not entirely satisfy Modyun. Which reminded him that time was slipping by.

"My solution to all this," he said, "is not to do anything to create further problems."

"That seems very sensible," said the woman.

Her reply was so good-natured that it seemed like a propitious moment to press his point. He accordingly recalled to her what he had said about the Nunuli regarding Earth as a conquered planet. "Long ago, before the human race was advanced to its present high state, that would have required me to declare war and drive the invader from our world." He confessed, "I do have the feeling that they gained their victory by a trick, and that such tricks show an abysmal, perverse character, which should not be allowed to succeed. But still—you'll have to admit that, as my animal friends would say, it's all water under the bridge."

"I agree," said the woman.

"So"—he completed his thought—"we'll have to live there a few days more as apes in order not to offend the hyena-men."

There was a small pause. The car thrummed along, its rubbery wheels singing. Then: "But I am not an ape," Soodleel said, with a peculiar intonation.

Modyun was mildly surprised at the reply. It seemed an obvious point, one that it would never have occurred to him to bring up himself. He did something, then, which he had not previously found it necessary to do: he mentally reviewed what he had said to her that might have evoked such a comment from her. And there was no question. His narrative had been singularly rational. He had clearly explained his predicament and the solution for it.

Soodleel went on, "You men have the strangest ideas. Obviously, the solution is that this time we arrive as human beings, and that ends the previous problem automatically. Let's consider that settled."

Modyun continued to sit beside her, unhappy. There had to be something wrong with her logic, but her voice had a note in it which implied that all communication on the subject was at an end. Since he operated on the principle of total respect for her—or any other person's—point of view, it *was* the end.

The silence between them was broken suddenly about twenty minutes later. Soodleel had been peering out of the window of the car. Abruptly, she pointed. "What's that?" she asked.

His gaze followed her finger. There in the distance a flat plain was visible through a canyon. Rising up from the plain was the largest structure Modyun had ever seen. Before he had time to more than glimpse its main outlines, the car had whipped past the narrow rift in the steep hills, and the monstrous thing was gone behind them. Nevertheless, Modyun had seen enough. "That must be the ship," he said.

He explained about his four animal friends, and their imminent departure for a distant star system.

He went on in a fond tone, describing how on the day of his sentencing the four had come timidly to his door to find out what the sentence had been. And of how relieved they were when they discovered that there was nothing in the wording of the penalty that forbade them to associate with him.

"So they've been eating with me," he said, "and visiting me. Except today, they're out getting the gear for the trip."

Soodleel made no comment about that, but she seemed neutral. It was a friendly neutralness. And so, later, when the car entered the city, Modyun pointed out various landmarks: the apartments for transients, the homes of the permanent city dwellers, a commissary, a street of shops . . . He was conscious of an expansive feeling. It bothered him presently that the feeling was one of pride, as if a person who knew such trivia was better than someone who didn't know. What surprised him, however, was Soodleel's interest in those very details. Yet, as was to be expected her attention finally went ahead to the residences which, long ago, had been reserved for human beings.

"Do you think they're still there unused?" she asked.

"We'll see," said Modyun. He pointed at a hillside ahead. "There they are to the right."

The house that Soodleel selected had terraced gardens that walked all the way up to the building, which was a series of five ovals that merged into each other. Each oval was a different color, and the overall effect was quite startling. But the woman liked it on sight. Since it was her idea to come to one of these places, Modyun did not argue. He identified himself to the car by his human name, and commanded it to deliver them all the way up the steeply sloping driveway to the front entrance.

After they climbed out, the machine drove off immediately. And there they were.

XI

THEY WERE definitely at the destination, but Modyun was still undecided. Should I accept her solution? he asked himself.

End his ape identity?

The Nunuli Master had warned against it. And what disturbed Modyun about that was, the alternative could mean animal dupes might be directed against the two human beings. They would then have to decide to what extent they used their defensive methods.

He half turned toward the woman to ask her if she had considered that. And saw that she was walking toward the pretty fence at the edge of the driveway. Beyond the fence, a cliff fell away steeply. And beyond that, stretching farther than he had previously realized, was Hulee. The woman leaned against the fence, and stared down and out at the scene below. Modyun remained where he was, but a good part of her view was visible from his vantage point also.

He now noticed something that had not been part of his earlier awareness. This was the highest house. The height of their hilltop gave them a sensational view; the best in all Hulee. Even the distant skyscrapers, like the one he had walked down from— their tops were lower than where he stood.

He thought: Maybe it isn't the color variety she liked, but the, height. If that were true, he was impressed.

It occurred to him that, as presumably the experienced human, he should be doing something.

What?

He looked around. The car had let them off opposite the front door. The driveway went on past, and then wound rightward out of sight behind the house. Obviously it made a full circle, for the vehicle had emerged farther down and had whipped back the way it had come.

He noticed something about the house. If it were already occupied, it didn't show. Near it, not a sound, not a movement.

56

Well, perhaps *some* sound. A mid-afternoon breeze rustled the bushes. Fallen leaves whisked across the timeless plastic driveway, noisily. A lark sang, startlingly loud.

Modyun went to the entrance. And was aware as he did so, that the woman had turned. He spoke his true name to the door computer—and Soodleel started toward him. Modyun pressed down on the latch. As the door unlocked, he gave it a push. Then, turning, he stepped toward the woman, and with a single continuous movement, picked her up.

Her initial weight surprised him by its amount, but he indicated additional strength for his muscles, and effortlessly, then, carried her across the threshold.

He was just a tiny bit breathless as he set her down, and steadied her while she recovered her balance. Soodleel said in astonishment, "What was all that?"

"It's the marriage ceremony," Modyun said calmly.

He explained how he had watched several dramatic shows on television during his period of confinement. He concluded, "It grew very boring, and I soon stopped. But an animal couple did that. So"—he shrugged, as he had seen Dooldn do on a number of occasions—"I learned a few details."

"So I'm your wife, now?" She sounded interested.

"Yep."

"Well"—she seemed uncertain—"I suppose under the new circumstances . . ."

"Definitely," said Modyun, "since we're going to be having sex."

She nodded, and turned away. "Let's see what our home is like after three thousand years."

Modyun did not object. He followed her from room to room, and it was all there pretty much as the teaching machines had described. Three bedrooms with adjoining baths. A hundred-foot living room. A large dining room. A study. Several small animal bedrooms, with their private baths, two rooms the purposes of which were not clear, and a commissary room with its automatic equipment.

One thing the machines had not conveyed: the beauty of the furnishings. The indestructible plastic materials of which everything was constructed, had been cunningly designed. Surfaces were shaped to give off a variety of light reflections. The effect was—anything the long-dead craftsman desired. Gleaming rosewood in one bedroom. An antique effect in another. The settees

57

in the large room were intricately carved of what seemed to be teakwood. In the same room were comfortable leather chairs and gorgeous Chinese rugs, and drapes that looked like tapestries.

The newly marrieds wandered from room to room, and Soodleel expressed herself as extremely satisfied. They had come to the commissary last, and she said, significantly, "We won't even have to go out to eat."

Modyun saw her point. But it seemed to him that it was an error for her not to realize the negative aspects.

The woman went on, "As you know, in growing like this we have subjected ourselves to some degrading necessities. Eating, and the consequent disposition of body wastes. Sleeping, with its time-taking quality. Having to stand and sit—it's all very distasteful. But, still, here we are. So at least we can do these things in the privacy of our own place."

Modyun temporized. "We must remember that the Nunuli probably knows now where I am, and may have learned that you are here."

"It is historically well understood," said Soodleel, "that these are not matters about which a woman should be concerned. Since we have reverted to a lower-scale evolutionary plane, you will no doubt take care of such details."

A great awareness dawned on Modyun. Soodleel had always been appreciated for her feminine point of view. And, evidently, she had had time to consider her new status, and she was manifesting the resultant philosophy. Interesting. Yet she was not taking into account that she would be as much affected by a Nunuli reaction—if any—as he.

The woman peered into some cupboards. Finally, content, she faced Modyun. "We've explored the house," she said. "What do we do next?"

Modyun explained that he had in mind their taking a trip around the world. But he had assumed they would wait a few days—his thought actually was to wait until his sentence was served, but he didn't say that. Soodleel listened patiently as he spoke these words, and then said, "Yes, but what's the next action today?"

Modyun was not exactly at a loss, then; he was simply adjusting to her instant need for something to do, and how to say it. "We could engage," he said, "in the same kind of philosophical thought indication as we do behind the barrier—"

She cut him off, with a tiny rejecting shiver. "Thought doesn't feel the same, with this body."

Modyun continued, "Or we can sit, or lie down, or read the animal books in the study, and then have dinner. And then maybe watch some television. And finally, of course, go to bed."

"You mean—just sit?" It was an amazed reaction. But even as she spoke it, she saw his face. And must have realized that this was a problem he had also had. She said slowly, "I sense in my brain . . . stimulation. It's as if all those neutral sections that control movement are affected by every sight and sound particularly, but also by the touch in my feet and the feel of the air on my skin. So far smell and taste make me draw back a little. But other than that I want to be in motion." She looked at him. "Well?"

Modyun was smiling tolerantly by the time she had finished. "You may have observed that these feelings intensified after you left the barrier. Beautiful though things are there, they are familiar; and so the neural pathways are long-established. But here" —he glanced around—"the house, the city, the people are all new and, even though ordinary, are stimulating. What you must learn is to become aware that these are body impulses, and the body must be controlled by the philosophically perfect mind."

He finished, "Meanwhile, close your eyes as often as possible. If that doesn't do it get up and dance like the animals. I've done it often during my confinement, particularly when certain music is played."

He could see from the expression on her face that his words had stimulated in her a resistant reaction similar to that which she had stated happened with smell and tast. He said quickly, "Perhaps, you have a suggestion"

"Why don't we try the sex," she replied. "That always takes the animals about an hour and a half—which will bring us to dinner time. We can decide after we eat what to do in the evening."

It seemed to Modyun an inappropriate moment for sex. Somehow, he had the impression that sex was a late evening or early morning activity. But he had already deduced that Soodleel's adjustment to a full-grown body was an extremely intense experience for her. So, fine, he thought.

As he led her through the longest oval to the largest bedroom, he said good-naturedly, "Historically, Doda believes that in the time before we ultimate humans, only a few saintly people could ever do without the sex act. Apparently, whatever the Nunuli did, it created in mankind that saintly—I presume the word correlates with philosophical—quality. Thus, we were able to make the changeover from animal-man to true man in ourselves."

As he completed that comment, another thought occurred. "Do your genitals," he asked, "resemble closely those of the female animal-people?"

"It's a comparison I have never made," said Soodleel, "on a close basis. Superficially, yes, is my casual observation."

"I took the trouble," said Modyun, "to examine a few females. I should be able to give you a fairly accurate analysis."

"Good," said the woman.

"Very similar," he reported a few minutes later. "Except"— he went on—"the animal-women manufactured a great deal of oil. I don't detect any of that in you."

"I notice," said Soodleel, "that you show no sign of the rigidity which was observable in all the males that we looked in on. Remember?"

"Perhaps, those phenomena occur as a consequence of activity," he said. "So we'd better get started."

The attempt at sex that Modyun now initiated presently puzzled them both. They rolled around in the bed, were slightly horrified at the physical contact of skin against skin, shuddered, shrank—but were determined, out of curiosity. Finally they lay back, and away from each other, baffled.

Modyun presently noted, "The animals seemed to be in a peculiar state of excitement. In fact, there was an unpleasant odor. We don't seem to have that excitement, and all I can smell is that ever-present, mild perspiration."

"When you were holding your lips against mine," said the woman, "you produced spittle, and it wet my mouth in a way that was very unpleasant."

"I thought it ridiculous to have dry mouth against dry mouth," justified Modyun.

Her immediate reply was not verbal. She moved over to the side of the bed, swung her tanned legs to the floor, and sat up.

She began to dress. In a minute she had on her trousers and blouse. As she bent to put on her animal-made shoes, she said, "Since that didn't take as long as I expected, I'll go for a walk. What will you do?"

60

"I'll just continue lying here but with my eyes closed," said Modyun.

Even as he spoke, she was gone through the doorway and out of sight. He heard the pad of her retreating footsteps on the thick carpet, and then the distant front door opened and shut.

Later.

As dusk settled, Modyun dressed, went into the commissary, and ate. Afterwards, mildly curious, he stepped outside and looked around for the woman. He could see the driveway winding down below him toward the city. Its entire length was not visible from where he stood, but the street lights had come on, and so he was able to establish that Soodleel was nowhere in his line of sight.

He recalled her objection to eating in a public commissary, and thought: She'll be getting hungry soon, and then she'll show up.

He returned into the house, and lay down as he had become accustomed to doing during his imprisonment. After several hours, it was time to go to sleep.

Still no Soodleel.

Well-l-ll, he thought . . . But he was tolerant. The woman was evidently exploring the city on her first day, beyond what he had done on his arrival. He remembered her need for motion. Evidently that need continued to motivate her.

He undressed, got into bed, and fell asleep.

Somewhere in the small, dark hours, the explosion occurred.

XII

AT THE split-instant of the cataclysm, all the human minds behind the barrier automatically indicated mass intermental communication on what to do. Modyun was unfortunately included in that intimate interrelation.

Everybody at once had indication-speed awareness of the threat and of the two alternatives: resist or not. And the incredible thing that happened was that no one but Modyun had a predecision on such matters.

His policy of passive acceptance of the hyena-men and Nunul ¡ rules was the only definite thought available. And during the fateful millionth of a moment when they still could have done something, that set purpose interfered with what might otherwise have been a natural reaction.

What that natural reaction would have been, was never to be known. The moment when something might have been done, came at the superspeed of basic Ylem reaction.

And was gone forever.

At the absolute penultimate moment, there was the faintest hint of a meaning, in which all those minds seemed to say, "Goodbye, dear friends" to each other. Then—

Instant blankness.

Moydun sat bolt upright in bed, and said, "Good God!"

By the time those words were actually spoken, millions of split-instants had gone by.

He must have leaped out of bed; must have turned on the light. Because when he came to his first awareness, he was standing in a brightly lighted living room. His second awareness was that his right leg was twitching, and that it was a weakening condition. Because his legs and thighs gave, he sank to the floor, sprawled on one side, kicking a little and trembling a lot.

By this time it was difficult even to see. The blur over his vision seemed to have its origin in a series of tensions that fed back from the body to the massive motor system in his brain.

For God's sake, what's happening?

He felt heat from an internal source. His eyes, his face, his body grew warm, then burning. It was amazing, automatic.

Water. He craved liquid; a goal that sent him stumbling to the commissary. The glass he secured trembled in his hand. He kept spilling the contents, as he lifted it to his lips. But he felt the cooling wetness of it running down his chin and onto his naked chest and then down his legs.

That wetness and coolness presently brought back enough of his reason for him to realize what he was feeling.

Anger.

That immediately gave him the biggest direction of all, an encompassing thought which grabbed at the free-floating sensation in his brain, and pointed it unerringly at the object of his feeling.

Because rage has movement in it, he ran back into the bedroom and flung on his clothes. The dressing was a kind of a stop. And so the fury built up in him. Then he was outside, running down the driveway.

It was as he reached the first roadway—and an unoccupied car was actually pulling over to him—that he had the belated realization that Soodleel's mind had *not* been involved at the instant of disaster. The puzzling reality of her absence remained with him all the rest of the way to his destination.

XIII

EXCEPT FOR the street lights and the brightly lighted buildings, it was still pitch dark as his transport vehicle pulled up in front of the computer center.

Modyun climbed out of the car relatively slowly. Time had gone by. And the overheated steam of his initial reaction had subsided considerably. He was even beginning to feel critical of the reaction.

Semichildlike responses, it seemed to him.

Nevertheless, he entered the building purposefully. Yet in fact he was not wholly clear as to what he proposed to do about what had happened.

The Nunuli who presently emerged from behind the machinery was not—Modyun recognized at once—the same as the one he had previously talked to.

"I arrived on Earth," said this new individual, in answer to Modyun's question about that, "a few minutes after the explosion, and came straight here. Which is what I deduce you did also—come directly here, that is."

The Nunuli stood in the open space in front of a little metal fence that was a guard rail for the giant computer machinery behind him. He was even physically different from the earlier one. Taller. Slightly more bent. Possibly older.

The discovery that here was a newcomer, who presumably was not directly responsible for what had happened, gave an even greater pause to Modyun's already dwindled ire. It suddenly seemed important to straighten out the confusion. "What happened to Number One?" he asked.

"He left," was the reply, "late last evening with the human woman."

"Before the explosion?" Modyun's voice reflected his surprise.

"Of course." Irritably. "A special agent of the committee arranged the explosion."

At last, the person he wanted. "And where," said Modyun grimly, "is he?"

"He departed approximately thirty seconds after the explosion." The Nunuli paused. "The timing of these matters," he continued, "was to ensure that none of us knew what the other was up to. The committee is noted for its unerring logic in such instances."

"Oh!" said the man. "And what is your role in all this?"

"I'm the replacement Nunuli Master of Earth."

It was all very baffling.

"This whole thing puts a strain on me, somehow," said Modyun. "I have the feeling that I ought to do something to you, personally."

If the Nunuli were disturbed by the implication of the words, it didn't show. He said testily, "For example, what?"

"I should probably subject you to some kind of penalty."

"Such as what?" asked the other, irritably.

"There's an old saying," said Modyun, "A tooth for a tooth."

"That would seem to me to be directly contrary to your philosophy. And besides," continued the alien impatiently, "what good would it do?"

"True," Modyun was nonplussed.

His feeling that he ought to do something was yielding rapidly to the obvious logic of the situation.

The Nunuli went on, "The fact of the matter is, they did not even try to defend themselves. Why should you now feel obliged to take any action?"

"Well!" temporized Modyun.

He had been thinking unhappily about his own role in the failure of the human beings to act. It was difficult to adjudicate such a complex mental phenomenon because, suppose he was *totally* responsible for their fatal hesitation at the crucial moment. Where would that leave him?

Among other things, it shifted the onus to some extent from the Nunuli over to him. And since that was clearly ridiculous, the truth was that—since the disaster was over and done with—blame had no place in the aftermath.

He found himself suddenly considering other aspects of the affair. "What motivated the committee to do such a thing" he asked.

"Number One told you. You threatened to become a nuisance."

"But that was me. That's not them. What would be the logic

5.

of striking at those who were not even considering coming out?"

"How would we know what they're considering? *You* came out." The Nunuli continued, "For all the committee knew, what's left of the human race could cause a lot of trouble. So they found the best solution."

"I suppose what you're saying makes sense, from their point of view," Modyun admitted reluctantly. "But you and their intent bothers me. The question arises: Should a being like you, who is associated with a committee capable of such a deed, remain free to do similar destructive acts of which you are obviously capable—since you have tolerated it in this instance?"

"What else is there that would be similar?" asked the alien being.

Modyun could only think of one comparison. "Your dupes, the hyena-men, have been harassing me. Which suggests that the previous Nunuli Master had designs on me."

"Hmmm!" The creature seemed to consider that. The bright, gray face lengthened a little. "Tell you what. All harassment shall cease. The remainder of your sentence is cancelled. You're free to do anything—go anywhere on Earth."

"It seems somehow an unsatisfactory outcome," said the man. "But I suppose it is the best possible under the circumstances."

"Very well. You are free to come and go—as an ape."

"So there is a restriction," said Modyun.

"It's very minor. What point would there be for the last human being on earth to announce his identity?"

Modyun had to agree that it would certainly not be very meaningful information. "But the fact is," he argued, "there is one other human being left: the woman, Soodleel. You say she left the planet last night?"

"The way the committee member, who dealt with this whole matter, reasoned it," said the Nunuli Number Two, "is that if only Number One knew where the human female was, and then he went off to some other part of the universe, never to return here, then it would be impossible for you to trace her."

Modyun stood there on the metal floor of the high-ceilinged computer center, and he could feel the vibration of all those suddering metal plates through the soles of his shoes. In his brain was another kind of impulse with its own intensity. He said finally, "It's an interesting problem."

"Unsolvable," said the Nunuli, with satisfaction.

The creature's triumph offended Modyun. But he recognized it as a body response, as if a part of him felt challenged to solve the problem. But of course that was not a truth. Why solve a problem that didn't have to be solved? Soodleel had left the house, and apparently had shortly afterwards gone aboard a vessel. The sequence of events was puzzling because his guess was that she had no plan to do such a thing. "Perhaps," he said aloud, "the simplest solution would be if you found out for me where she is, and told me."

"Out of the question." Curtly.

"What is your motive for such a refusal?"

"You are a male. She is a female," said the Nunuli. "It would be ridiculous for us to permit you two to mate and produce off-spring. So she's gone where there are no human men, and you're here."

Modyun dismissed the possibility that Soodleel would ever permit the reproductive process to come to fruition. His attention accordingly went to another thought. He said, "Number One was actually able to seize her and put her aboard some vessel?"

"Well—no!" The being's almost glass-smooth, grayish face rippled with some kind of internal muscular, and perhaps emotional reaction. Modyun analyzed it as a kind of smug, amused superiority. "She was very trusting, according to my report," said the Nunuli, "and naturally would not violate my predecessor's mental privacy. So, when he invited her to visit one of the committee's swift ships, she went aboard without suspicion. Even after she felt the vessel lift, it was later reported by the commander that she remained unconcerned."

Modyun was relieved. "Well, of course," he said. "One place is as good as another. This is something you people do not seem to grasp." His interest was now fading rapidly. He said, "I see now that your intent was to cause her and me damage, but fortunately human thought transcends your evil and makes nothing of it in this instance. So Soodleel is on a ship being taken to a specific place. At some future time when you come to a better awareness of reality, I would appreciate your finding out for me where she is."

"I repeat, that will be never," was the reply.

"I assumed you might say that," said Modyun. He turned away, indifferent. "I have a slight responsibility to her, so I may persist on a future occasion."

"It would do you no good," said the new Nunuli Master. "I don't know where she is, and the committee has issued specific instructions against such information ever being given to me. So I couldn't help you even if I wanted to. Which I don't. That should complete our discussion. Unless you have another question."

Modyun could think of nothing.

XIV

OUTSIDE AGAIN. Still dark. But dawn was a faint glint now in a cloud-filled sky. Modyun walked along the sidewalk, which was deserted. The street, of course, was alive with cars. All that he saw were unoccupied, but what *should* they be doing at night except keep moving in case somebody wanted to utilize their services. That was what they were for.

Three things bothered him. One was that he wasn't exactly sure how he should feel. Second, he observed that his body was not in good spirits. But his third awareness was that intellectually he was relieved.

He realized that Soodleel had been a strain on him. Suddenly, with her arrival, the positivities of another being had had to be taken into account. And after only a couple of hours she had begun to be quite wearing.

Someday no doubt they would get together and discuss the future of man. But it scarcely seemed urgent.

I suppose right now I ought to go to bed and give the body its needed sleep. Then in the morning I can decide what to do next.

As he flagged down a car, it occurred to him that he was no longer interested in making the world tour. Since it was to have been for the benefit of those who remained behind the barrier . . . no point in that now.

So what next?

Bearing in mind the one restriction that the Nunuli had imposed—to keep his human identity secret (and why not?)—he directed the car toward the transient quarters. Then, leaning back in the seat, he thought: A member of the faraway committee took a direct interest.

Incredible. Yet stated to be so by the Nunuli.

A direct interest in a small planet (Earth) in a dimly populated —in terms of numbers of suns—outer edge of the Milky Way galaxy. He realized that what he was actually trying to imagine was the idea of a conspiracy against two individuals: Soodleel and himself. It *seemed* impossible.

A committee member might advise the Nunuli, yes; *if* advice were asked for. But their general directive surely covered such infinitesimal (by their standards) entities as himself. The Nunuli had merely tried to be thorough—as good servant races should.

A single human being, a pacifist philosopher, harmless in that he was *totally* willing to let live, and who never struck back, such a person would not be of the slightest interest to a ruling, conquering galactic hierarchy. At this enormous distance, they would not normally even know that he existed as an individual. And any advice they gave their creatures, the Nunuli, would not concern itself with who, specifically, it was for. That was the way it should be.

In spite of the perfect logic, he couldn't quite bring himself to make a final acceptance of his reasoning.

I'll think about it again, later.

He had descended from the car by the time he reached that point in his thinking. As he came within sight of his little apartment he was astonished to see that the bear-man, Roozb, was sitting on the veranda steps. The handsome animal-man half dozed against one of the supporting beams.

As Modyun came up, the animal-man opened his eyes, blinked, and said, "Hey!" His voice was loud on the night air. He must have noticed how loud for as he leaped to his feet he almost whispered. "Where have you been? You got us all worried."

The human being explained quietly that something had come up requiring his attention. By the time he finished, Roozb had him by the arm and was tugging him toward one of the other apartments.

He pounded on that door and, when a sleepy Dooldn opened it, he thrust Modyun at the jaguar-man and rushed off, calling over his shoulder, "I'll get the others."

In five minutes, they were all assembled in Dooldn's apartment. And Roozb was growling in his deep voice, "Fellows, this ape isn't all here"—he tapped his forehead—" 'cause he broke his confinement rules only two days before his sentence was up. By tomorrow, there may be hell to pay, and we won't be here to help him."

He turned to Modyun. And his handsome face was grave as he explained that all four of them were scheduled to go aboard

70

the interstellar ship this very morning, before noon. Takeoff was scheduled for the following morning.

Modyun was surprised. "You mean—they expect to get a million people aboard in one day?"

Dooldn interjected, "In an emergency they could. But they didn't. They've been loadin' 'em for two weeks. We'll be among the last fifty thousand to go aboard."

Roozb waved his friend silent. "Never mind gettin' off the track," he said. "Question is, what're we gonna do about this ape? He doesn't seem to know the ropes."

Across the room, the fox-man stirred. "I got it. Why don't we take him along?"

"Ya mean, out to space?" The bear-man was startled. Then he shook his head. "That's probably illegal."

"Illegal by whose standards?" chimed in Dooldn. "Only the usurping hyena-men." He shrugged. "Nobody'll notice an extra ape among so many. An' he can just say they musta lost his papers."

It was an awed hippopotamous-man who turned and stared at the human being. "Hey, Modiunn, what do you think? Like to go?"

What interested Modyun in what was happening was their willingness to conspire on his behalf. Amazingly, that one thought which he had presented, the concept of usurpation, had eroded their loyalty. First Roozb's and Dooldn's, and now, apparently, with the passage of time, Narrl and Ichdohz had also been— what was the word?—corrupted. For just a few moments the veil had been torn aside. Still not knowing the real truth, they had responded to the lesser revelation with anger and a deterioration of their previous innocence and purity of purpose.

His thought went back to his fellow criminal, the rat-man, who had been impelled to steal when he learned that the hyena leaders were driven that extra hundred yards to their front doors. A privilege which he resented.

It really doesn't take much, Modyun thought.

The perfect balance that man had left, when he retreated behind the barrier, had been disturbed by the conquering Nunuli. Too bad. Maybe something should be done about that.

He grew aware that all four pairs of bright eyes were still eagerly fixed on him, waiting his response. It reminded him of something else he should do first.

71

"I'll be going out at dawn," he said. "But I should be back here by nine or nine thirty. Would that be too late?"

They assured him earnestly that it wouldn't.

What he did at dawn was drive out to where Eket had brought him nearly a month ago—and where he had met Soodleel. He had a mental picture of the terrain and of a possible route over which the car could take him across the roadless country. As he had anticipated, the robot auto obeyed his human name.

And so, presently, Modyun stood on the hill overlooking what had been the valley where the thousand had dwelt in their paradise. Everything was gone: the gardens, the interlinked canals and pools, the golden homes and grounds which had formed a circular core about a mile in diameter. Also missing was the outer fringe of dwellings where the insect and animal attendants of the human beings had had *their* homes.

Where the little city had been, with its remnant of the human race, was a gouged-out hole three miles long, two miles wide, and half a mile deep.

If he were to go out into space, maybe in one of the days ahead he could have a talk about all this with a member of that committee . . .

Abruptly it seemed like something that, in fact, ought to be done.

XV

MODYUN WAS not at first concerned with locating a permanent room for himself. After separating from his four friends—they had their assigned quarters to go to—he sauntered along a corridor and found himself presently at a gate overlooking a huge open space.

His eyes swiftly measured the place to be well over a kilometer in diameter and at least a hundred meters high. Everywhere he looked were trees, and a vista of grassland, and of course thousands of animal people enjoying the pleasant outdoor effect. It seemed like an ideal place to spend his first few hours aboard. Modyun stepped forward to go through the gate—and found it locked.

An animal-woman came forward. She was neatly dressed, and had the appearance of being—well, of all things—an ape. She looked up at him from her height of seven feet three inches to his eight, and said, "These compounds are rationed, sir. With so many people aboard, the open spaces have to be used in stagger fashion. If you give me your name and room number, I'll see that you are notified of your time to come here."

It was an unexpected condition, but reasonable. Since he had no assigned room, Modyun shook his head no at her suggestion. But he was studying the ape-woman with genuine interest. "What part of Africa?" he asked.

"East coast." She smiled in an attractive way. "Where the good-looking ones come from," she said. "Would you like to share my quarters?"

Modyun was definitely curious. "How could that be arranged?"

She was smiling delightedly at his apparent willingness. "If a female can get a male, she's entitled to a large bed. There's several in every dormitory."

"Seems like a good idea," said Modyun. "Where?"

"I'll write it down for you," she said eagerly. He watched her as she hastily took a little notebook out of her purse and wrote several lines of fine script on it. She tore out the sheet and handed it to him. "Here."

Modyun accepted the note, glanced down it, and read, "Deck 33, Section 193, Corridor H, Dormitory 287." It was signed: Trolnde.

He placed the paper in his breast pocket. The ape-woman said, "What's your name?"

He gave her the African spelling, Modiunn, and said, "I'll see you at sleep time."

In due course, evening came. Then late evening; and it was time to go to the address Trolnde had given him.

Modyun was awakened during the night by the ape-woman rolling over on top of him as he lay on his back. She was fairly heavy, and so, after considering the possibility of letting her remain there without comment, he rejected silence, and said in a low, courteous voice, "Are you awake?"

"You bet I'm awake," she said in an equally low voice.

"Is this a typical sleeping habit of the apes from your part of Africa?" he asked.

"For God's sake," she said, "what kind of a question is that? Are you a man or a nothing?"

It seemed an obscure question. So he said, "Why don't we discuss riddles like that in the morning? Right now I'm pretty sleepy."

There was a long pause. And then, without another word, the woman rolled off him and over to the far side of the bed. Presumably, she remained there, because he slept without further interruption. When he awakened in the morning, Trolnde was already up and doing something on the far side of the dormitory where there was a mirror.

Modyun started to dress. And he was in the act of bending over and putting on his shoes when he felt the floor under him shudder. It was instantly such a massive event; so much power was obviously involved, that an indication took place in his brain without his conscious direction.

Pictures flitted through his mind.

He saw, first, just waves and undulations in a contained space. It was a visual world of quadrillons of moving lines.

Magnetic-gravitational, he thought. And, of course—that would be the way. The ship would have to interflow with the enormous magnetic and gravitational fields of Earth in order for its gigantic bulk to break away from such a mass.

74

So this was takeoff. Very easy. Direct. Nothing threatening.

With that relieving awareness, the pictures . . . changed. He saw a hyena-man face: a uniformed officer with medals in a great room somewhere on the ship. The room glittered with mechanical devices, and other uniformed hyena-men stood before paneled instruments.

The scene faded; and for a fleeting moment the gray-smooth face topped by the wormlike hair of a Nunuli superimposed. The creature's eyes, like limpid pools of gray-green mist, seemed to gaze directly into Modyun's.

And then that faded also.

Modyun completed putting his shoes on, and realized that he was pleased. Now that they were spacebound he could go eat. He had agreed with the others that he would remain away from the commissary the entire previous day. He had done so, but for a body like his it was quite inconvenient. That would now rectify.

He climbed to his feet and walked over to the ape-woman. "See you again tonight," he said cheerfully.

"Don't you dare come back here," said the ape-woman.

Modyun, who had been turning away casually, faced about and stared at her. "I detect a distinct hostility in your tone," he said. "Which surprises me, since I treated you with complete courtesy."

"I don't need that kind of courtesy," was the grim reply.

It occurred to him that her irritation was related to her mysterious behaviour of the previous night. He reminded her. "Is that it?" he asked.

"It certainly is," she replied with asperity. "I expect a man to behave like a man when he's with a woman."

"Oh!" said Modyun.

Understanding was a glop in his mind. He protested, "Do you believe in crossbreeding?"

"Who was going to breed?" she snapped.

It was an obscure answer. But he was remembering his abortive experience with Soodleel. He said, "Actually, there's a problem I have to solve. So why don't I consult with some friends of mine, and then talk to you again?"

"Don't bother," said Trolnde coldly.

She was clearly not in a reasonable mood. Modyun accordingly gave up on the discussion, and departed. He headed straight for a commissary that he had seen on his way to her quarters the

75

previous night, gave the computer his real name, and shortly was carrying a plate to a small corner table. He ate what was on it in a leisurely fashion. As he did so, he became aware that hyena-men in uniform were lining up outside each of the four entrances to the commissary.

Modyun sighed. All that foolishness will now start.

He was conscious of a new thought for him: How much more of this shall I tolerate?

The feeling faded as a hyena-man, wearing more than the usual amount of gold braid, entered the commissary and walked over to him. "Is your name Modiunn?" he asked politely.

"And if it is?" said Modyun.

"I respectfully request that you accompany me to the quarters of the Nunuli Master of this ship."

The overheated emotion somewhere inside Modyun cooled considerably at the tone of the polite request. It didn't evaporate completely, but his automatic courtesy was triggered. He said, "What does he want?"

"He wants to ask you a few questions."

"I," said Modyun, "cannot imagine a single question of any value that he might ask to which my answer would have any meaning. So the answer is no, I will not accompany you."

The hyena-man was suddenly confused. "But," he protested, "how can I take back a message like that? For all I know, he would expect me to use force if persuasion failed. Though I have no instruction to that effect."

Modyun said with dignity, "Convey to this gentleman that if he wishes to assign me a cabin aboard this vessel, and then cares to visit me there, I shall receive him."

The hyena-officer seemed relieved. "Thank you," he said, "I needed a message of some kind."

He departed.

That was all there was. The hours went by, and no reaction. It seemed odd. But then, Modyun reflected, the Nunuli were schemers, and no doubt some plan was going forward as it had in connection with his confinement on Earth. Though it was difficult to imagine what. Finally, since he had nothing better to do, he went up to visit his friends.

Their address turned out to be a dormitory like Trolnde's— except all men. At first survey of the large room with its tiers of bunks, there was no sign of the four he was looking for. Modyun walked over to a bunk bed, where a mouse-man and a somewhat smaller-than-Narrl fox-man were playing cards, and asked about his buddies.

The immediate reaction was unexpected. The mouse-man dropped his cards onto the bunk, leaped to his feet, and yelled in a shrill voice at other men in the nearby bunks. "Here's a guy looking for those four so-and-sos!"

About half the men in the room heard those words. And everyone of them stood up. And individuals in remoter bunks, attracted by the commotion, looked around, or sat up. A few made it to their feet.

From Modyun's left, a burly person whose face faintly resembled that of a tiger, motioned at him preemptorily, and said, "Come over here, you!"

Modyun, though puzzled, nonetheless did as he was bidden. From behind him the mouse-man shrilled, "They've been arrested. And we've been instructed to question anybody who comes and asks for them. Who are you?"

XVI

THESE ARE dupes, thought Modyun. That was what was so instantaneously severe about the situation. He turned automatically, with that realization, and looked back toward the door through which he had come.

But the way was already blocked. In those few moments, between the mouse-man's first yell and his response to the tiger-man's preemptory command, seven individuals had moved between him and it. So the peaceful retreat from an area of possible violence, which was a part of his perpetual peace code, was no longer the solution.

Modyun resigned himself to the inevitable confrontation.

It was a swiftly rowdy crowd. Even as he stood, undecided, creature-men pressed around him, pushing each other and him. And what was immediately unpleasant about that was the smell of animal sweat in close proximity. Nevertheless, it did not occur to Modyun to shut off the odor. Nor did he resist the way they began to press him into a corner. That was an expected part of his initial failure to leave the scene.

Somewhere in there, the tiger-man hit at Modyun's face. It was a glancing blow, which was diverted to a point higher on his head. The pain of it was minor, but the intent galvanized him. He said, "What was that for?"

"You're a dirty stinking so-and-so, that's what," was the reply. "And we know what to do with traitors and their friends, don't we, fellows? I say, kill the so-and-so!"

The cry was taken up by those nearby. "*Kill the so-and-so.*"

With that, several hard blows struck Modyun's shoulders and head. He backed away from his attackers unhappily aware that his body would undoubtedly defend itself when the pressure became great enough. So he indicated no-pain for himself, put up his left arm to ward off their fists, and because he was to that extent impregnable, struck the tiger-man on the jaw. He felt the blow as an impact on his knuckles that reverberated back to his shoulder socket. No pain, but a jarring effect.

78

Because there *was* no pain, and he had no experience, he hit without the slightest hold-back. And then watched in dismay as the animal-man reeled a dozen feet. The big man fell to the floor with a crash.

Everybody—but everybody—turned to look. They also were inexperienced. And so they took their hands off of Modyun. And their attention. They stood there, gaping at their prostrate friend.

It made an opening; not precisely physical, but an opening of temporarily no-purpose. Through that opening, Modyun weaved. It had to be a weaving motion, because a round half-dozen persons were in his direct line of motion. Past these nonactives, he penetrated, bent down, and assisted the dazed tiger-man to his feet. "I beg your pardon," he apologized. "All I wanted was a chance to ask you a few questions."

The big fellow was recovering rapidly. "You sure pack a mean wallop," he said with a note of respect. "Questions?" he repeated.

Modyun expressed himself as being astonished by their hostile attitude. "Since when," he said, "has it been a crime to know someone?"

The words gave pause to the tiger-man. "Well . . ." he said doubtfully. Then he turned to the roomful of animal-men. "What do you think, fellows?"

"But it's criminals he knows," the mouse-man pointed out.

"Yeah." The tiger-man glared at Modyun, abruptly more belligerent. "What about that?"

"You say they were arrested?" Modyun said.

"Yeah. You bet they were."

"Taken into custody?"

"That's right."

"Then they're still to be put on trial. They haven't been proved guilty of anything." Modyun remembered his own appearance in "court," and added quickly, "They're entitled to a trial by a jury of their peers—that's you fellows. A dozen of you and a judge in a properly assembled court in the presence of the public —that's the rest of you—listen to the evidence against the accused, and determine if it proves what the prosecution contends."

He broke off, "What are they accused of?"

Nobody knew.

"Well," said Modyun scathingly, "you ought to be ashamed of yourselves, all of you. Judging a man guilty without even

79

knowing the crime." His own part in the unexpected development grew clearer. "Fellows," he said, "we've got to make sure these four people—who are just ordinary people like you and me—get a fair trial."

They were only animal-men, and kind of simple. And they had been left a perfect world, which required a minimum of work from them. In a way, the direction provided by the hyena-men and the Nunuli had probably been good for them. Pushed at them. Given them something to think around. And more to do.

On such people—he had already noticed—anything that was obviously fair made an immediate impression. So it was now.

"You're right. That's what we've got to see to." It was a general chorus of agreement. Animal-men turned to and re-assured each other earnestly of the validity of the long-unused principle of a just trial.

With that, the roomful of people broke up into small, excited discussion groups. No one seemed to notice when Modyun edged his way nearer the doorway by which he had entered and, after a cautious survey, stepped outside.

He walked rapidly off down the corridor, disturbed by what he had learned of the mysterious arrest of his friends, but at least free to do something about it.

What, was not exactly clear.

My problem is, I'm a philosopher. It was a new idea for him, to think of it as a problem.

For a while after that, he walked on and on in blankness. But it was a mental blackout. His speed of walking increased auto-matically, reflecting his deep inner upset. The speedup in motion presently focused his attention on that aspect.

Then, finally, once more, he realized . . . on the body level, I love those four. And their predicament disturbs me—on that level.

He began to run.

Faster.

As he raced along, his heart beating more rapidly, his breath coming in gasps, he was aware of the charged-up emotion—about what had happened to his animal friends—slipping away. It had been, he realized, a chemical feedback from certain over-sized glands that, since his growing into size, had taken over a good portion of his reactions. Pretty sad to realize that such glandular injections into the bloodstream—adrenalin among them—could be dissipated by muscular activity.

As he ran, the feeling that he ought to do something, disappeared.

A philosopher again, he smiled at the earnest concept that had almost involved him in a matter that was really none of his business.

It was an old tenet of the peace lover that the madness of the violent people had no end. So never get involved. Make no counter moves. Avoid reacting.

Let them win.

Easy winning softened aggressors. True it was sometimes inconvenient, but still if you could avoid getting involved afterwards, or as little as possible, it was better to keep the peace that way. Even if a few people got hurt, it was better.

With that reaffirmation of his most basic truth, Modyun slowed back to a walk.

He was hungry now. He entered the very next of the numerous commissaries that he came to.

It was while he sat eating that he saw the same small drama—as that morning—of hyena-men in uniform lining up outside each entrance of the large, busy place. And then the same high-ranking officer respectfully approached him, and handed him a document.

Its exterior looked very similar to the summons he had received back on Earth. And Modyun was conscious of an instant, intense heat starting somewhere at the base of his spine. He recognized the body rage, and said hastily, "What's this?"

"You are to appear as a witness against four persons accused of illegally bringing an unauthorized individual aboard this vessel. Their trial begins tomorrow morning at nine o'clock in the location named in the summons."

Not just each sentence, but each partial sentence the hyena-man spoke, was sensationally revealing. Modyun's reaction was to each word. He kept saying, "Oh. Oh. Oh." And it was invariably an "Oh!" of dazzled comprehension.

The mystery of the arrests was solved.

Evidently, on Earth, spies had spotted the four as being associated with him. So, the moment, he—Modyun—was discovered aboard (undoubtedly reported by the commissary computer), somebody had analyzed that his friends had played a role in bringing him onto the ship.

Difficult to guess what such a trial would accomplish. But no

6   81

doubt the Nunuli Master was up to one of his devious games. The sly underlying purpose would eventually emerge from what was happening.

The hyena-officer said respectfully, "I have been asked to secure your promise to appear as a witness as ordered."

Modyun hesitated. But truth was, what else could he do? His own systematic thought required that he let the villains have their way. By winning without a fight, they would be appeased . . . his philosophy argued.

Nevertheless, he remembered his exhortation to the animal-men an hour before. And, though the accusation didn't seem to be too serious, and was probably only a part of a bigger scheme against himself, he asked the decisive question: "Will it be a trial by jury and judge?"

"Yes."

"You're sure?" Modyun persisted. "You understand what that means?"

"A judge and twelve jurors will consider the evidence, and the accused will have a defence attorney assigned them."

That certainly seemed to be it. "All right," said the human being, "I'll be there."

"Thank you." Whereupon the officer reached into his pocket, drew out another folded sheet, and held it out.

Modyun gazed at the paper doubtfully. "What's that?" he asked.

"I was told that if you agreed to be a witness, you would be assigned a cabin—as you requested this morning. This is the cabin number and location."

Modyun took the paper with considerable relief. He had been wondering where he would spend his second night.

He said, "Please convey my thanks to the Nunuli Master. Tell him that I appreciate his courtesy."

As promised, the trial began promptly at nine the next morning, and the first witness called was Modyun.

XVII

THE COURTROOM was arranged exactly as he had pictured it from the description of the teaching machines.

The dozen jurors, all hyena-men, sat in a jury box along one wall. The hyena-man judge sat on the bench in his robes. The witness chair, to which Modyun had been called, was just to the left of the judge. The hyena-man prosecutor sat at one of the tables to the judge's right, and the hyena-man defense attorney at the other. Directly behind him in a special enclosure sat the four defendants, with hyena-man police officers lined up behind them. Directly opposite these various legal apparati, beyond a low fence, were several dozen rows of seats. In these sat the members of the public.

With the setting so perfect, it was somewhat jarring to have the prosecutor climb to his feet and say without pause, "This witness is named Modiunn. He is an ape from Africa, and he was brought illegally aboard this vessel by the four accused. This is a crime of treason, sedition, and otherwise a capital offense, punishable by execution of all four guilty parties."

He had been, as he spoke these words, addressing the jury box. Now, he turned to the defense attorney, and said, "What is the witness's plea to this vile crime?"

The defense attorney without rising said, "The witness admits all of these statements as being true. Proceed with the trial."

"Objection!" roared Modyun at that point. His body was warm from head to foot. He was vaguely amazed to realize that he was trembling.

"Objection overruled," said the judge in a courteous tone. "The defense attorney has spoken for the witness."

Modyun yelled, "I object to this travesty of a trial. If it continues in this fashion, I shall refuse to be a witness any longer."

His Honor bent toward the witness chair. He seemed puzzled, as he went on in the same courteous tone, "What fault do you find with this trial so far?"

"I demand that the witness be questioned directly and that he shall be allowed to answer the questions himself."

"But such a thing is unheard of," protested the judge. "The defense attorney, being familiar with the law, is obviously more qualified to answer for a defense witness." A new thought seemed to occur to him, for his eyes widened. "Oh," he said, "you're from Africa. Is what you are requesting the common procedure there?"

Modyun drew a deep breath. He was startled at the number of mental operations that were required of someone who had to take account of more than the simple truths that Man had come to live by. But he refused to become involved in anything more devious than lying about the spelling of his name. That plus his false identity as an ape was *it*. Beyond that, only the truth.

He said, "I demand that court procedure follow the rules set up by Man."

There was a long pause. Finally, the judge beckoned the prosecuting and defense attorneys to his bench. The three held a whispered conversation. Finally, the two lawyers returned to their tables. When they were seated, the judge in his polite voice, addressed the entire courtroom, saying, "Since this witness's testimony is important, we have decided to accept the somewhat primitive procedure to which he has become accustomed in his home country of Africa." He now turned to Modyun, and said in a chiding tone, 'I sincerely hope that afterwards you will apologize to the defense attorney for the insult to which you have here publicly subjected him." He continued courteously, "How do you wish to be communicated with, Mr. Modiunn?"

"The proper procedure—" began Modyun.

"Where you come from," interjected the judge.

"—As long ago established by Man," continued Modyun, "is for the prosecuting attorney to ask me a series of relevant questions, and each time wait for my answer."

"What kind of questions?" asked the hyena-man on the bench, obviously willing but visibly puzzled.

"He should begin," said Modyun, "by asking me my name."

"But we know your name," was the amazed reply. "It's right here on this summons paper."

"Such facts must be established by direct questioning," said Modyun firmly.

The judge was doubtful. "Such a method could keep us here all day."

"Perhaps even a week," said Modyun.

There was a gasp from just about everyone in the courtroom. And His Honor, politeness momentarily forgotten, snapped, "Impossible!"

Yet, after another pause, he spoke to the prosecutor, saying, "Proceed, sir."

That hyena-man came forward. He seemed uncertain. Nonetheless, he did ask the basic questions: "What is your name?" "Are you in fact an ape from Africa?" "Are you the person who is accused of being aboard this vessel illegally?" "Do you know what crime the defendants are accused of?"

It was to that question that Modyun offered his first resistance, taking on—in doing so—a sort of combined witness and defense attorney role.

XVIII

"I OBJECT to this question because what the defendants are being accused of is not a crime by the laws of Man as established before they retreated behind the barrier, leaving the rest of the Earth to their friends, the animal-men."

So argued Modyun. He went on: "If it is an offense by any definition, it is strictly a minor one, the penalty for which should be possibly confinement to quarters for two or three days at most."

As he reached that point in his argument, he was interrupted by the judge—who ruled that the accused were guilty of a capital offense by definition.

"Definition?" said Modyun.

"Yes, definition," was the answer.

"Show me the definition," objected Modyun.

The clerk of the court, a scholarly looking hyena-man in a shining black suit and high shirt collar, brought out a book in which in Chapter 31, page 295, paragraph 4, line 7, began the words: ". . . shall be deemed a capital felony, punishable by heavy prison and or fine, or death."

"Let me see that," said Modyun. The clerk surrendered the volume, after glancing for confirmation at the judge, who nodded. Modyun reread the lines, then turned back to the fly leaf, read what was there, glanced up triumphantly, and said, "This is not a Manmade law, but a false and unacceptable modification by a minority group—the hyena-men."

"I," said the hyena-man judge, "declare it to be relevant and applicable." His voice tone was distinctly less polite.

"In my opinion," said Modyun, "you should find the accused innocent on the grounds that no offense has been established."

"My only question to you," said the judge, "is: Are you going to testify or not? If not, please step down from the witness box." He spoke acidly.

It seemed scarcely the moment to withdraw, so Modyun said, "I'll testify—but I reserve the right to bring up this matter again."

The judge turned to the hyena-man prosecutor. "Continue with your questioning of this material witness," he said.

"How did you get aboard this vessel?" the prosecutor asked.

"I walked across the dock to one of several hundred entrances. I entered an elevator. It took me up something over a hundred stories, and I stepped out of the elevator onto and into a corridor. It was my belief at that time that I had safely arrived aboard the ship, and this belief turned out to be correct," concluded Modyun.

There was silence in the courtroom as this factual account was completed. The long, lean hyena-man who had asked the question, seemed nonplussed. Yet, he presently rallied, and said, "Will you look over there to the prisoner's dock?"

Modyun looked as directed, and of course saw his four animal friends.

"Do you," asked the prosecutor, "recognize any of those persons?"

"I recognize them all," said Modyun.

The prisoners stirred audibly. Narrl seemed to sag down in his chair, almost as if he had been struck.

"Order in the court," yelled the judge.

The prosecutor went on, "Were any of those persons"—he waved at the accused—"over there, present when you walked across the dock, entered that elevator, and came aboard the ship?"

From where he sat, the human being could see that the animal people in the general seats had become tense. He sensed that many of them suspended, or slowed, their breathing involuntarily, apparently anticipating that his reply would be in the affirmative. Modyun turned toward the judge. "Your honor, I perceive that a great deal of importance is being attached to my answer to this question. It is as if everybody is automatically assuming that a yes answer would be damaging to the prisoners. Would this also be your consideration?"

The long, thin creature leaned across the bench towards him. "As a witness," he said in an advisory tone, "it is your duty merely to answer the question truthfully. What conclusions I may make in my final judgment, will be determined by the logic by which judges operate."

"Still," objected Modyun, "you are a member of the minority group that has usurped these various positions, including derogating to hyena-men only the right to conduct trials and sit in judgment. Therefore I have a suspicion that your judgment might not be entirely unbiased. If you can convince me that it will be unbiased, I shall gladly answer the question."

"It will be unbiased," said the judge.

Modyun shook his head. "I'm afraid we're not understanding each other. Anyone can make a statement of unbias. But how can you convince me, in view of your being a member of a usurping minority, that you will not prejudge these prisoners."

"I'm afraid," said his honor coldly, "that I'm going to have to ask you again either to testify or step down."

"Oh, I'll testify," said Modyun.

"Very well. What is your answer to the question?"

"The prisoners in the dock were with me when I entered the ship."

"Aaaaaaaaaaaaaah!" said the audience. They seemed to respond as one person. It was a sighing sound, as if many people had taken the opportunity to resume breathing.

The judge was banging his gavel for order. When there was finally silence once more in the courtroom, Modyun said to the jurist, "You see, I detect an assumption which, in effect, judges the association of the four prisoners with me as being significantly against them."

"What other assumption can there be?" asked the judge, scarcely concealing his triumph.

The human being stared at him pityingly. "The assumption that my accompanying them was not related to the charge against them. The assumption that, although they were with me, they didn't necessarily know my intent." He made a gesture. "A dozen similar assumptions."

His Honor motioned to the prosecutor. "Proceed with the questioning of this witness, and pursue those particular points that he has brought up. He seems in the end to answer truthfully, so obtain the truth from him."

It was a good point—Modyun had to admit. Though he might reason philosophically about the truth, the fact was he was not about to lie about actual events. So the prosecutor pressed from him one admission after another. Finally: yes, the four accused did know in advance that it was his intention to go aboard the interstellar expeditionary ship. Yes, indeed, one of the accused had suggested it, and the others had agreed.

When Modyun had finished, the judge glanced at the defense attorney. "Any questions of your witness, sir?"

88

"No," was the reply. "In fact, I see no point in wasting time with any continuation of this trial."

"I agree with you," said the judge.

He thereupon turned to the prisoners. "Stand up!" he commanded.

The four accused climbed uncertainly to their feet.

The judge continued. "Your guilt having been established by this witness—" he began.

"Hey!" said Modyun, loudly.

The judge ignored him and went on firmly. "I hereby order all four of you to be taken to your cell—"

"What about the jury?" yelled Modyun. "This is supposed to be a jury trial."

"To be held there for one week, pending an appeal to a higher court. If such is not granted, exactly one week from this day you four shall be put to death by a firing squad using N-energy weapons."

He waved at the uniformed police who stood in the dock with the prisoners. "Take the condemned away," he ordered.

He now turned to Modyun, and said in a courteous tone, "I want to thank you for your honest evidence, which established beyond all need for further red tape that the four accused are indeed guilty as charged."

"Wel-l-ll," said Modyun, doubtfully.

XIX

HE HAD done what he could—so it seemed to Modyun. Nothing else to do now but let due process take its course.

Yet all of the rest of that day of the trial, his body remained unpleasantly warm. Which of course was a glandular foolishness not to be tolerated by the philosophically perfect mind. What was particularly ridiculous about his body's attachment to Roozb and the others was that he had met them quite accidentally.

It isn't as if I sought them out for some special quality that I observed in them.

On the day of his emergence from the barrier, he had flagged down a car with four occupants, and taken one of the two spare seats. And that was the whole sum of the meaningfulness of the meeting. There was no difference between those four in that car and any other animal-men.

That, he argued to himself, was the real perspective in his relationship with them.

And still his body remained warmer than normal.

The fourth morning after the trial, the buzzer on his door made its humming sound. When Modyun opened the door, there was the uniformed hyena-man officer, respectful, and with the information that "The four accused have had their appeal turned down by the higher court. As the chief witness, the court insisted that you be advised of this verdict."

Modyun was about to say thank you, and was about to close the door, when it occurred to him that his face had flushed scarlet at the news. He said hastily, "I desire to visit the condemned before their execution. Can this be arranged?"

"I shall be happy," said the officer, "to make an inquiry on your behalf, and I shall advise you of the decision."

It turned out that he could, and that he would be permitted his visitation on the eve of the execution—the evening of the sixth day after the trial.

They are very obliging and legal about the whole matter,

Modyun had to admit. His earlier feeling that there was some devious scheming in all this, aimed against him, seemed to be completely in error.

From the outside, the prison cell simply looked like another dormitory, but with a barred door leading into it. In front of the door sat a hyena-man guard. This individual carefully read Modyun's written authorization for the visit, and then unlocked the door for him, waited until he had entered, and then locked it behind him.

Several moments went by during which time the place looked deserted. Suddenly, a pair of legs emerged from the interior of a lower bunk—and Narrl sat up with an exclamation that sounded for all its muffled quality like, "For Pete's sake, look who's here!"

Those words hastily produced three other pairs of legs, and three familiar individuals emerging from as many other lower bunks. All four animal-men came to their feet, walked over, and shook hands with the visitor.

Glancing around, Modyun saw that there was, in fact, a difference between this and the other dormitories. Because, beyond the furthest line of tiered bunks was an alcove. And there were the tables and familiar equipment of a commissary.

Modyun said diffidently after his brief exploratory look, "Thought I'd better come and say good-bye."

A great big tear rolled down Roozb's cheek. He seemed pale, and not very good-looking: kind of hollow-cheeked. "Thanks, pal," he said in a choked voice.

Modyun stared at him with considerable amazement. "What's the problem?" he asked. "Everybody's got to go sooner or later. So why not right now?" He corrected himself, "Tomorrow, that is."

There was a silence after he had spoken. Then Dooldn came and stood in front of him. There were two enormous pink spots in his cheeks. He swallowed, and evidently was restraining himself, for he said, "Boy, you sure think strange." He frowned. "Modiunn, I never met an ape like you before. There you sat in the witness chair, telling on us."

"Truth is truth," defended Modyun. At that point, it occurred to him that the remark that the jaguar-man had made was not entirely friendly. "You're not mad what happened, are you?" he asked.

The pink spots began to reduce in brightness. Dooldn sighed.

91

"I keep intending to be as mad as hell at you for that. And then I think, 'Well, that's my lovable lame-brain ape pal, putting his foot in his mouth again'. So then my anger becomes helplessness. Right, fellows?" he glanced around at his companions.

"Right," said Narrl and Ichdohz gloomily. Roozb was silent, staring at the floor, and wiping his eyes.

Their point of view was so lacking in perspective that Modyun felt the need to reeducate them. "How old are you?" he asked each in turn. And discovered for the first time that their ages ranged from twenty-six to thirty-three: Roozb being the latter age, and the hippopotamous-man, the former. Since they were animal-men, their life expectancy was about sixty. "So," Modyun reasoned, "you've all lived roughly half your normal lifetimes. The remaining half scarcely seems worth fighting for."

This argument was given an unmixed reception of blank stares.

It was the fox-man who finally made an emotional statement. "To think that I'm here in this terrible predicament because I tried to be your friend."

The human being was startled. He couldn't see how there could be any relation between the two conditions. "You're suggesting," he said, shocked, "that there is such a thing as cause and effect. That's not true. You did what you did. Then the hyena-men did what they did. The two events are not related in a rational world. It's something in their heads that says there's a connection. There is no connection, in fact."

Modyun saw that his words were not being understood. They simply looked downcast, and seemed unhappier than ever with their fate. He felt a sudden pity, and continued:

"What you should be aware of," he said, "is that life has no meaning that anyone has ever been able to discover. So each species should narrow itself down to a small group in which each individual carries within himself all the bundles of genes—that is, the entire genetic heritage—of the race, and wait."

He went on, "Since there are plenty of each of your species back on earth, there's no reason why you should hold onto your particular repetitive existence. In fact, there's a good possibility that in this voyage of conquest you would get yourselves killed anyway."

The guard pounded on the door, as those words were spoken. "All visitors out!" he yelped through the barred window of the metal door.

"One moment," Modyun called. He turned to his friends. "Well," he said, "what do you think?"

A great big tear rolled down Roozb's cheek. "Goodbye, pal," he said, "I don't know what you're talking about, but I think you mean well." He held out his hand.

Modyun sighed, as he had seen Dooldn do. "I have to admit," he said, "if that's the way you feel about it, then you'd better come with me when I go out. No use your going through with something that you're resisting so hard. I'll tell the authorities that you consider the sentence unacceptable. That's correct, isn't it?"

The four animal-men were staring at him. The jaguar-man was pitying. "How can we come out with you?" he asked. "The armed guard is right there."

The human being gestured, dismissingly. "I'll just indicate a suitable by-pass—some minimum interference with his mental rights—and we can resume this discussion in my cabin."

Naturally, he thought, there will be some repercussions. So maybe, now, I'd better go and have that talk with the Nunuli Master.

It was approximately an hour after the four had accompanied him to the cabin, that the door buzzer sounded. And when Modyun answered it, there stood the uniformed hyena-man complete with the braid of his high rank. He whispered to the human being, "I am once again instructed to ask you to come and have an interview with the Nunuli Master. Will you come?"

Modyun stepped out into the corridor, indicated an energy barrier as a protection around the cabin, and said, "I'm ready to go this instant."

He closed the door behind him.

XX

He followed the hyena officer along a corridor, and thought: I've got to prove to the Nunuli how illogical that trial was.

As they went up an elevator, up, up, it seemed to Modyun that life was going to be awfully complicated if he had to protect four animals and himself during the entire rest of the voyage. As they walked across an open space from the first elevator to another one, he thought: Let's hope the Nunuli has an acceptable solution.

After the second elevator stopped, the hyena-man briefly watched the control panel. When a white light began to blink on it, he pressed a button. The door slid open on its silent mechanism; and the hyena-officer said, "You will enter by yourself. This is to be a private conversation." As Modyun stepped forth, the door closed softly behind him. He did not glance around but walked out into a room not more than a dozen feet square. The room was bare, except for some kind of covered mattress on the floor. On this, lying on his back, was the Nunuli.

Modyun saw at once that it was a different Nunuli from the two that he had previously met on earth. Which of course was natural. They would need one individual on a ship such as this and, of course, another one on Earth. At least one in each location if the committee's work was to be done.

"You find me," said the alien on the floor, "at a time when I am resting from my numerous duties."

Modyun took another look around, seeking an exit to another room. Or something. There was nothing visible to his cursory glance. "These are your quarters?" he asked.

"Yes."

"This is your home aboard this vessel?" Moydun persisted.

"Yes." The tight, gray skin of the long face seemed to change a little, as if a picture from within was trying to form on it. However, it was the picture of a thought-feeling and not of a scene, and so it was a little difficult to evaluate. The Nunuli continued, "You find these quarters perhaps more ascetic than the cabin which I assigned you?"

"I was merely interested," replied Modyun, "in establishing the fact of a situation. It would seem that your committee requires its chief agents to be without personal interest in luxuries or other tokens of power."

Again, the face of the being on the mattress, altered. An expression appeared fleetingly, which was similar to one that Modyun had observed on the countenance of the second Nunuli Master of Earth, which at the time he had interpreted to be a superiority smile. The alien said, "We were already an ascetic race when the committee selected us for their high purpose. All we have ever required was—" He stopped, then muttered, "Never mind what."

"No doubt," nodded Modyun, "your species had arrived at the correct ultimate conclusion that everything in the universe equals everything else in the long run. So why acquire worldly goods beyond the simplicities necessary for minimum survival. Is that it?" he asked.

"No."

Having spoken, the Nunuli continued to lie down. And, after several seconds, it became obvious that he had no intention of enlarging on the matter. Modyun accepted the refusal without rancor, and said, "I respect your privacy."

"Naturally," said the Nunuli. "The human race was improved by us to manifest exactly such respect for the rights of others. We observed this quality in them and developed it with the intention of creating a lop-sided effect. This was achieved. So there are no surprises in your statement."

Modyun said, "I sense within myself that nothing is quite as automatically one-sided as you analyze. For example, I find myself irritated by your logic in connection with the trial of my four friends."

"You don't know what my logic is," was the retort.

"True. But, still, it seems obvious. You have subjected to trial four animal-men from Earth, because of some role that they played in my coming aboard this vessel."

"What's illogical about that?"

"The ship was constructed on Earth, was it not?" asked Modyun.

The Nunuli seemed surprised. "Yes, of course. We always use the local factories and materials, where possible."

95

"And your workmen were Earth animals?" persisted Modyun.

"Naturally. Who else? The committee insists on local labor being employed."

"Then," said Modyun, "what could your argument be? By definition I am entitled to be on this ship."

"I don't understand your reasoning," was the cold reply.

Modyun spread his hands. "Earth belongs to Man, and in a lesser degree to the animals that man raised from animalhood. Therefore, this ship, which is of Earth and made by Earth animals, belongs to Man and to a lesser degree the animals. I am the only Man aboard, so this ship belongs to me."

"Earth is a conquered planet," said the Nunuli with dignity. "Therefore, Man owns nothing of it or from it."

Modyun stubbornly shook his head, and he felt his eyes narrow ever so slightly—a body phenomenon which rather amazed him, for it seemed to be a kind of emotional bracing against the other's point of view. "I am not yet reconciled to the Nunuli takeover," he said. "Until I am, the ship belongs to me. However"—he broke off—"these are minor aspects. I have been considering the best solution for this situation. I am searching for a female human being, whom I have reason to believe a colleague of yours had removed from Earth and transferred somewhere else. If you can take me to her, I'll be glad to leave this vessel wherever she is.'

"That solution is quite impossible," said the creature on the floor. "But now let us return briefly to your logic. The error in it lies in your unawareness of another purpose that we had in connection with you. Do you realize how many days have now gone by since the departure of this vessel from Earth?" His tone had an aspect of glee in it.

"Slightly over a week," said Modyun. He was, he had to admit it, puzzled by what seemed an irrelevant question.

The creature was calm again, the gray-green eyes fully opened, the gray, tight-drawn face skin slightly less taut. "This ship," he said, "has now proceeded approximately 400 light-years. It has altered course several times, and has deliberately overrun its target so that in making its approach no clue remains as to which direction it originally came from."

The Nunuli paused as if to give Modyun an opportunity to react. Since it was visibly expected of him, the human being finally expressed himself as being baffled by the information. "Though, of course," Modyun analyzed, "it is no doubt wise to give your potential enemy no data as to the planet of origin of the attack vessel."

From the gleam in the other's eyes, he deduced that he was not getting the picture. And, in fact, after a moment of obvious gloating, the creature explained, "What you say about our target planet is undoubtedly also true. But the ship's evasive tactics were entirely for your benefit. Designed to confuse *you*. To make sure that *you* never returned to Earth. And that, also, was the intent of the trial of your animal friends. If you'll think about it, you'll see that we kept your attention diverted until the last possible moment by the trial and their fate during the decisive period while the ship was covering the necessary distance. Naturally, this vessel will not return to Earth."

So that was the scheme. It all seemed slightly unnecessary to Modyun. But then the logic of a subordinate agent race like the Nunuli was probably always extreme. These people had a mission to accomplish in connection with Earth. So now, having achieved the destruction of the human beings behind the barrier, and the removal from Earth of Soodleel and Modyun, that mission was presumably accomplished, by their lights.

The total irrationality of the mission and its underlying goals, left Modyun with the feeling that, really, what could he say to such madness? Except, he could point out a logical consequence.

"In that event," he said, "since my four friends were merely pawns, you will have no objection to cancelling the execution judgment against them, and grant them full pardons."

"No objection whatsoever," was the instant reply. "Indeed, that's one of the things I called you up here to tell you."

He went on in a more formal tone, "Redddll, the hyena officer who brought you here, will accompany you back to your cabin and will present each of the four with a certificate of clearance."

Still lying on his back in that bare room, the Nunuli concluded, "It seems to me that that should complete my communication with you at this time."

That seemed true to Modyun, also. Except for one or two things. "Are your schemes against me now completed?" he asked.

"How do you mean?" The being on the floor seemed puzzled.

"The pattern has been: something is done against me, I accept it. I even tolerate the particular Nunuli who conspired to achieve that something. The whole matter passes out of my mind. I continue with my peaceful existence. And then I discover that a further conspiracy has been proceeding against me. So I want to know—are there any more? Conspiracies, that is. Or does this one complete your mission in regard to Earth and human beings?"

"It is now completed," was the reply. "What else could there be?"

"That's what Nunuli Master Number Two said," answered Modyun, "but it turned out to be a lie. And I'm getting tired of all these lies and schemes. They go against the basic truth of the universe."

"How could the last member of any race possibly know basic truth?" the Nunuli said irritably. "But let me consider." After a pause, he continued, "The only other purpose we could have with you in the frame of our mission would be to kill you and the woman. In your opinion, is there any way in which this could be achieved?"

"Well, no." Modyun spoke after a moment of considering the matter, himself. "Not if I resisted."

"All right"—still irritably—"then you have your answer."

On the surface, it certainly seemed a satisfactory and truthful reply. And yet—

"There is one thing," said Modyun, "which is so important that it may require me to indicate a reply from you."

"That," said the Nunuli, "would be intolerable."

The meaning of the words shook the human being; because, of course, to do something intolerable to another person was unthinkable.

Yet—after a moment—he continued to think about it.

Modyun said, "I have come to realize somewhat belatedly—" He stopped, and allowed the meaning of his own words to penetrate the inner sanctum of his mind. The meaning was not reassuring because here he was the last survivor, other than Soodleel, of the human race. And so his awareness of the truth—if truth it was—had come late indeed. It was not wholly obvious what he should do about it . . . but a conversation with the committee, first—yes.

He completed his statement: ". . . realize somewhat belatedly that it may not be wise for one race to allow itself to be improved by another whose motives may not be altruistic."

Even as he spoke, he could feel the old, modifying feelings making their voiceless communications from somewhere in the groin of his nervous system. He heard himself say, "This matter is not settled with me. These are simply logical conclusions of an interim nature—"

It required a conscious effort to stop the words. He stood for a long moment, amazed at the power of those feelings. But presently he had them under control, and he was able to say, "Whenever I talk to a Nunuli, I find myself listening to a reaction to my words which is little more than stereotyped duplicate of what was previously said by another Nunuli. And so I am compelled to ask: How may I determine that the Nunuli are, or are not, themselves the committee which they purport to represent?"

He broke off, "On something so basic you can see that I shall have to overcome my natural reluctance to indicate, unless"—hopefully—"you have a less drastic solution."

The pale eyes of the Nunuli were staring up at him with such intensity that Modyun, after a long moment, said unsteadily, "Why don't you open your mind to me of your own free will, and show me enough of the history of the Nunuli race to establish that it is not, in truth, what I suddenly wondered about?"

Below him, as he finished, the creature stirred. The thin legs shifted. The arms twisted a little. The neck bent back as the creature sat up.

"Very well," it said, "I yield to your criminal pressure. But I warn you that the committee may be offended, and I cannot answer for their subsequent actions if they are."

XXI

THE PICTURES that began to come were of a simple, ascetic life: Nunuli, presumably on their home planet, living a monklike regimen. There were views of long, dark buildings, where each of the creatures had a tiny cell-like room in which to live his drab existence. The floors were bare, and the cell unfurnished except for a sleep pad.

Other views showed Nunuli women in slightly different-shaped buildings. The difference was that in these were communal yards and rooms, where children were tended, and in their early years kept in comfortable crib-like structures.

Once every few years a Nunuli woman would set out purposefully one morning, and seek out one of the monasteries. The mental picture that came showed her knocking at a cell door. Then at a second door. Then a third, and so on. The male in each cell apparently recognized the knock, for he got up from his pad, and opened the door. There he would stand gazing at her. There she would stand, waiting. She seemed undisturbed by the initial rejections, but simply walked onto the next cell. Finally, in every instance (of the three that Modyun watched) she arrived at a room where a male was attracted by either her odor or by a thought wave that came from her. With this accepting suitor she would remain several days and nights. Mostly, the two simply lay side by side, meditating. But twice during her stay would come a moment. An excitement? Even with his good mental contact, Modyun wasn't sure exactly what the feeling was. Whatever it was, it impelled a copulation that seemed to go on interminably. Four hours. Five. Certainly, most of a night.

After the second such, the female simply got up, and without a backward glance at her mate, departed from the cell and from the monastery. She was next shown back in her own little cubbyhole, with other women in the background. There in the silent secrecy of her cell she gestated and in approximately a year gave birth to a peculiar little monster who presently began to take on the Nunuli appearance.

All the scenes faded abruptly. On the floor of his small apartment, the Nunuli Master looked up at Modyun and said, "That was our life before the committee showed us the way of service."

Modyun said, in surprised disappointment, "That's all you're going to show me?"

"That summarizes our pre-Zouvg history," was the tart reply. "Precisely what you asked for."

Modyun opened his mouth to protest that it was not a sufficient reply. And then he paused. Standing there, he realized that he had just heard a remarkable revelation.

Zouvg—the Nunuli had said.

The context implied that it was the name of the race of the committee . . . I really must have had him under pressure, to have gotten such information. For several long seconds he relished the word. Finally it struck him that what he had originally intended to object to, was still important. He said, "What you have shown me doesn't explain the jump from a severe, monastic existence to galactic-wide mass murder. How did that transformation come about?"

The green-colored eyes stared him, puzzled. "Are we discussing the same subject matter?" the Nunuli began. And stopped. "Oh!" he said. His eyes widened as if with a tolerant understanding. "What we do on behalf of the committee," the alien said, "is not murder."

"Let me," Modyun said, "clarify this point. You or some other Nunuli destroyed, or connived in the extermination of, the human race. By the credo you operate by, that is not murder?"

"That"—The Nunuli made a dismissing gesture with one slender, smooth-gray arm—"is part of the program of the committee to improve the life situation in the galaxy."

"To improve what?"

The creature was calm. "I'm sorry. I must now ask you to do me the courtesy of leaving me so that I may continue my period of rest. Your problem is resolved. Your friends are safe. You have the information for which you asked. You surely do not intend to pursue this matter any further against my definite objection?"

Modyun hesitated. The words did not seem to affect him as he ordinarily would have expected. There were still several thoughts in his mind, and—disturbingly—an actual impatience with opposition.

"I seem to be in a strange mood," he said finally, "I have several questions I want answered." He did not wait for the Nunuli's permission to discuss the matter, but went on, "I guess the most important is, how do the committee members gain the support of persons like yourself?"

The blue-mist eyes seemed to become slightly puzzled. Then the smooth face tightened into what for want of a better term might be called a frown. When he spoke it was with an "of course" attitude. "They're a superior race. The moment one of them contacted us, he implanted a purpose. Since then, after we've looked over an advanced culture planet and we decide that we need subtle methods, we call on a committee member to implant purposes in the minds of key individuals. That's it. All resistance ends."

Modyun said, "Oh!" a light had dawned. "Purpose," he said, "Of course."

He asked pointedly, "When the Zouvgites contacted the Nunuli was it a thought communication? That is, was it a mental conversation that resulted, a dialogue?"

The Nunuli was indignant. "A committee member," he said, in an outraged tone, "does not discuss anything with a member of a lesser race."

Modyun restrained his triumph. It was a small victory, but he had learned something that the Nunuli did not know. What the Zouvgites had was not two-way thought transference, in the usual meaning. They could apparently place the entire energy of their brains behind a purpose.

A purpose could be almost anything. In that sense two Zouvgites could transmit purposes at each other, presumably could defend themselves against the hypnotic impact of each other's transmission, and could thus safely converse across the miles and years of space by way of the Ylem. Similarly, a suggestion (purpose) could be transmitted to other person—who had no defense against it.

Modyun was amazed to realize that his body was trembling from the information. It cost him an effort to say, "Can they . . . combine . . . behind a, uh, purpose?"

"All thousand of them," said the Nunuli, with satisfaction. "Irresistible."

That completed the picture of that quality of the Zouvgites. Against such a defensive one-way lineup of a thousand individuals, each one of whom could put up a massive delaying resistance, the human indication method could not be used directly.

He was abruptly anxious to know other things. "The purpose of these people," he said, "continued to puzzle me. Their plan to improve the galaxy has included the elimination of the human race and presumably other species. What is the scientific reasoning behind that?"

The Nunuli was matter-of-fact. "That information is classified. I know, but I cannot reveal it."

The fleeting thought came to Modyun that four billion men and women of Earth were dead as a result of the Zouvgite purpose; and at least he ought to know the rationale. "On a point like that," he threatened, "I may have to indicate."

"It wouldn't do you any good," said the Nunuli. His manner was complacent. "I've been assured that no one, not even a human being, can penetrate the special condition in my brain which guards that data."

"It might be an interesting test," said Modyun, "for you and me to discover if that is really true."

But he spoke half-heartedly; and he detected within himself an acceptance of the l imitations which he had laid down earlier; that if the Nunuli revealed his back history, there would be no forcing. Somewhere inside him that seemed an incredibly binding agreement. Which was pretty ridiculous, since—in time of emotion or strain—he did use the method regardless of previous moral commitments.

He said now, thinking thus, but still hesitant: "What did the Zouvg say is the nature of the barrier in your brain?"

"If you used the indication system in that area," was the reply, "it would kill me instantly."

"Oh!"

"It was, and is, taken for granted," said the Nunuli calmly, "that you will do nothing that will actually harm me. In the final issue, you will show compassion."

"I suppose that's true," said Modyun reluctantly. "But still—"

He explained that this—the biologic—was an area of which human beings had complete knowledge. "What we have done for Earth animals is only a tiny aspect of our total ability to manipulate cells and cell groups. I have already observed that you have, not the same, but a comparable type nerve cell to that of human beings. Each of your nerve cells has a long connective thread of nerve tissue coming out of either end. In human beings the comparable connectives are called axons and dendrites—"

"I am familiar with the anatomical details you are describing." Curtly.

"Good. At one time on Earth,'' Modyun continued, "it was thought that the axon was simply a single line like a telephone wire, capable of carrying an electrical impulse, the same with the dendrite. However, it was found that each of these minute threads of nerve matter is dotted with from five to ten thousand little spots. Subsequent tests established that every single one of these dots was itself an output or input terminal. So imagine the original human brain with about twelve billion cells, each with nerve ends possessing anywhere from five to ten thousand inputs and outputs, none of which is apparently being used in direct transmission of brain impulses."

"I am extremely familiar with these details," was the tart reply. "It was our advanced observation of these special terminals, which other races lack, that made possible our improvement of the human species to a level where each individual had complete power but was restricted from utilizing it against others by a philosophy—you may recall?"

Modyun recalled it unhappily. But he persisted with his reasoning out loud.

"In an operating electronic instrument, unused inputs and outputs create noise. In the human brain, they were a source of confusion and misassociation. However, it was subsequently discovered that the inputs actually received *all* the thoughts of other people, and the outputs actually transmitted the entire content of the brain into the Ylem. But—and this is my point— what came in and went out was so charged up with noise, it wasn't possible to isolate the information until the indication system was developed.

"I can't see anything particularly wrong with total power being restricted by a philosophy—except (it's beginning to dawn on me) where it works towards total self-destruction. Which means I feel fairly free to indicate. I *think* I could very easily help you by-pass or nullify the barrier programming inside you . . ." Modyun let the sentence hang. "But," he concluded, "what I really want is more information"

There was a long pause. The strange eyes had become fixed as they gazed up at him. Finally, the Nunuli said, "I'll answer almost any question but that. I'm not sure that what a committee member does can be overwhelmed by your knowledge. What else would you like to know?"

"Where is Zouvg?"

"I don't know. I've never been there. Obviously, they wouldn't have anybody close to you who did know."

That seemed immediately true to Modyun, also. He said, "Then summarize for me what you do know about the committee."

"They are the most advanced race in the galaxy. What science they did not develop themselves, they took from other races by their method of mind-control. They are the only truly immortal species—"

Modyun interrupted, "You mean, the longest-lived?" He smiled. "Man lives about thirty-five hundred Earth years at present. There is a possibility that evolution will eventually bring this up to about ten thousand. There is a reason why at that time a normal cell fades into a more shadowy state, which in effect is death."

The smooth, enigmatic face was blander than ever. "I repeat, true immortality. Several committee members are more than a hundred thousand Earth years old. Do you hear that?"

"B-but that's impossible at this stage of galaxy evolvement," Modyun protested, "except in one way." He was disturbed. "Long ago, we human beings decided not to pursue such an unnatural way."

"You failed to pursue it because of your philosophy—correct?"

"Basically, I suppose so. But also because—"

He was cut off. "That was your error," was the calm reply. "Nature does not worry about right or wrong methods. Only the fact of the situation matters. The fact is that they are all immensely old individuals, and you are not even capable of what they have achieved." The being on the pad broke off. "Surely, you will now end this interrogation, and we can go our separate ways."

"Yes," said Modyun. "The rest I will get when I have a conversation with a committee member. Could you arrange such a meeting?"

"Impossible—for reasons which I have already explained. They don't accept communications. They only give them—in the form of orders."

"If it ever becomes possible," said Modyun, "you know where I am."

"Indeed, I know where you are," was the reply, spoken in a tone of satisfaction, "and where you are going."

"Where's that?"

"Nowhere."

XXII

IT WAS over.

There were outwardly at least no further problems for the animal-men. The four were nervous when they first returned to their dormitory. But when nothing happened—when, in fact, their dormitory companions crowded around them and clapped them on the shoulders and shook their hands (there were even a few cheers)—they quickly resumed their carefree existence.

But they had very definitely had a severe experience. The extent of the shock they must have been in, was revealed the first time they returned to Modyun's cabin. When Modyun, who had been in his bathroom, came out, he found them gazing around the place in envious wonder. They seemed to have forgotten the hours they had previously spent there. They examined, and exclaimed over the sumptuous living room. Next they peered into the magnificently furnished bedroom. But it was only when they saw the kitchen with its private commissary that their amazement became vocal.

"Boy!" said Roozb, his head tilted suspiciously. "This is really rating. How come?"

"Yeah, what gives?" asked Narrl, his sharp nose pointing inquisitively, his head tilted.

Ichdohz and Dooldn stood by, their eyes round and curious.

Modyun gave the explanation that had been suggested by the high-ranking hyena-man. "The way it was explained to me," he said, "when I moved in, was that since I was not scheduled into one of the dormitories, there was no other place for me but one of the spare officer's cabins."

"Boy!" said Roozb, "it sure pays to be a stowaway."

Modyun continued generously, "Why don't you fellows come in at mealtimes and eat in here with me? That way we'll keep in touch."

They readily agreed. And so he had companions for his next few mealtimes. Which was somehow pleasing. Not that they were

107

great company for him. Because now they began an almost incessant chatter about the forthcoming landing. It became the inescapable subject. When they would depart for some additional training instruction, and Modyun would turn on the closed-circuit TV, there'd be heavily braided hyena-men sounding off on the same matter. Only one channel carried music during these preparatory hours, and it was not always the same one.

On the second day, the four arrived at his apartment each with a packsack and a long instrument which radiated a quiescent charge that registered on one of the indication systems in the human being's brain. Modyun examined one of the weapons, and saw that it was not of Earth origin or design. "Very ingenious," he said, as he handed the weapon back to the jaguar-man, its owner. The now-familiar two bright pink spots appeared in Dooldn's cheeks. "You kidding?" he said. "Took days to get the operation of that thing through my noodle. And you act as if you got it already."

"Well—" said Modyun.

"Probably saw 'em before in Africa," interjected Roozb from across the room. "Right, Modiunn?"

Modyun was happy to make that explanation. "This looks like the ones I saw in Africa," he said glibly. "The charge is in this long bar." He indicated a shining extrusion, which lay lengthwise along the bottom of the barrel of the riflelike weapon. "When you press the button at the top here with your thumb, the bar releases its charge like a battery. From the size, I'd guess that the energy that instantly flashes forth could transform a column of air of about five hundred yards into a conducting state. And so the electric current from the little dynamo inside the stock arrives at any intervening target without loss. My guess: a thousand amperes at 660 volts—enough to kill an unmodified elephant." He shook his head, sadly. "Too bad."

"What's bad about it?" That was Dooldn. "We may need something like this for defense down there. Who knows what we'll run into?"

Since they were unaware of the real purpose of the expedition, Modyun let the matter drop.

It was during the meal that they now ate together that he discovered that the landing was scheduled for the following morning, shiptime.

XXIII

MODYUN, at the request of the Nunuli Master of the spaceship, remained in his room. Under the circumstances—the creature pointed out—it was the least he could do. That seemed reasonable to Modyun. He accepted that, in a way he was an intruder, and should therefore remain as unobtrusive as possible.

His request—that he be allowed to view the landing on his room viewplate—was curtly turned down by the Nunuli. Modyun's body—he observed—was piqued by the refusal; but fact was it was none of his business. And, of course, it was likewise true, that a take-over such as this would be extremely boring with innumerable repetitious actions.

Modyun did not trouble himself to imagine what was going on below. The continental land masses that he had glimpsed in the early stages of the ship's approach were of sufficient size to justify the conclusion that there were large numbers of inhabitants; and he presumed that these beings were being subjected to a predetermined method of take-over.

He followed the usual routine required by his full-grown human body. As that day's sleep period approached, he ate a light meal. Then, while he relaxed, waiting for the body's toilet needs to manifest, he allowed his body to listen to some lively animal music. Strange how the blood seemed to course a little faster, the heart beat swifter, the eyes shine. It continued to be a source of education for Modyun, a possible explanation for human behavior of the old days, that such excitements and stimulations were so easy to evoke.

We really come from a pretty primitive type, he thought. Rather startling to realize that it was that primitive human whom the Nunuli had found—and unerringly analyzed to be vulnerable to a certain kind of conquest. Which, of course, was meaningless. After all, what they thought they had achieved, and what they *had* achieved, were two different horses.

By the time he was having these thoughts, Modyun completed

his private degradation of the toilet, stripped off his clothes, and climbed into bed.

It was an hour later, when there was a knock on the door—awakening him.

A knock, he thought. What's wrong with the buzzer? But he turned on the light and climbed out of bed. "Who is it?"

"It's me, the Nunuli Master of the ship. I want to talk to you."

"Why not come back after the sleep time?" asked Modyun sensibly.

"What I have to say can't wait."

Modyun's reasoning was at once in conflict with his natural courtesy. His reason said that obviously that was not so. The truth was, that if he and the Nunuli *never* had another conversation about anything, it would be no loss. And, of course, also, no gain. But he had always been kind even before reason. And that was true now.

He said, "I'm naked. Shall I get dressed before I answer?"

"No, no, it's not necessary. I'm always naked, as you know. Your body is ugly, but I can stand it."

Look who's calling who ugly, thought Modyun as he walked to the door and opened it. The Nunuli entered with a slithering movement, and with surprising haste. Hurrying over to the bed, he sank down on it.

"We're having a little problem below," he said. "I was wondering if you might give me the benefit of your reasoning."

"What's the problem?" asked Modyun. He was making no promises—yet.

The Nunuli got up off the bed. "Perhaps, you could get dressed, and come down with me."

"Now, I get dressed—now I don't. Make up your mind," said Modyun.

"Get dressed. The temperature below is near freezing. We seem to have come down on a cold part of the planet."

As he put on his clothes, Modyun had a thought, and finally offered it as his opinion that it would be unwise for him to leave the ship for any reason. "After all"—he pointed out—"I'm aboard without your permission. For all I know, once I got down there, you would simply order the ship away from this area of space, and I would be marooned here. And I really don't even know where 'here' is."

"I thought you didn't care where you were," was the sharp reply.

"My body is getting tired of being fooled by simple devices," Modyun said, "and I have very little interest in the confusion you keep trying to create."

The Nunuli seemed to resign himself to the human being's objection. He said succinctly, "The battle below is going against us, and I am therefore requesting that you use one of your indication techniques and save the army down there."

Modyun was astonished at the other's false picture. He pointed out that the indication techniques were strictly limited, and were not any use at all in a mass situation. "They provide," he said, "a limited control of the elemental forces in a specific space. Any time that you Nunuli really wanted to kill me, you could probably do it. But you'd have to be prepared to have the forces you use backfire on you personally. That's the way it would work."

If a cluster of wormlike appendages and a glass-smooth face could be said to have a faraway expression, then that was the way the Nunuli reacted to his explanation. The alien seemed pensive, but finally said "What would be your method of handling an attack by the enemy on the ship itself?"

"Get your men aboard, and leave," said Modyun, simply.

The other confessed, "It's a problem which I myself have never faced, and I must admit that I'm baffled that I could have analyzed these, uh, Gunyans so inadequately on my previous visits. I could have sworn that subtle techniques were not needed, and that we could just come in with our power crowbars and smash the place up." He explained, "That's always the simplest method. It does the job right now, and it's out of the way. We install our subordinate government and await instructions from the committee." He shook his head. "Not like your Earth. Remember? There, confronted by the existence of an atomic civilization, we had to adopt a method that required several hundred years."

He abruptly remembered his purpose. "The situation is very serious. Even you may shortly be inconvenienced by Gunyan energy blasts, if you don't give us some help."

There was an earnestness in his manner that carried conviction. "Exactly what has happened?" Modyun asked.

A pause, then frankly: "Our landing craft are immobilized," said the Nunuli, "and a large Gunyan force—perhaps the equivalent of two divisions—has taken over the entire rear section of the ship, including the big park there. They did it by a method which is not obvious to me and my technical advisers."

"Possibly," nodded Modyun, "that's where I could be of assistance. Why don't you and I visit the rear section? I presume you're now willing to abandon this attack?"

"Yes, of course." The creature seemed distraught. "But first we must disengage and reembark our ground forces. A good two hundred thousand men are down there."

Modyun was impressed. "That's certainly a large number, and presumably it includes my four animal friends. They told me that the drawing-by-lot method had selected all of them."

"I wouldn't know anything about such details," said the Nunuli hastily.

Modyun, one hand on the door, turned and frowned at the alien. "The way you said that"—he spoke slowly—"makes me wonder about your 'lot' system. Could it possibly be on the same level of integrity as the hearings back on Earth were as to the destination of this vessel?" His eyes narrowed. "Is it possible that my special friends were deliberately chosen, and were assigned to most dangerous tasks in the hope that they would suffer injury or death?"

"No, no, I swear." The Nunuli was flustered. "There could be no point." He paused desperately. "If your friends are down there, the sooner you intervene, the better. I can assure you it's a total nightmare. Something has to be done, or the entire force will be wiped out."

"I can't quite imagine what I can do," said Modyun, "but since the purpose is stop the attack, let's go and see."

With that, he opened the door and stepped out into the corridor. The Nunuli followed close behind him.

XXIV

ALMOST AT once, they had a hard time moving.

Swarms of animal people were coming from the rear. There were squealing sounds, and the clump and clatter of feet as men and women anxiously pressed toward the forward part of the ship.

"Stay directly behind me," Modyun urged the Nunuli, as he interposed his larger body between the fragile alien and several large animal people hurrying toward them, pushing at them and past them as if they were not there. It was a mindless throng essentially unaware of the two persons attempting to go in the opposite direction. Fortunately, it was uneven in its masses. Sometimes, there was a considerable empty space where the terrified were merely approaching. During such moments, the two—the human and the Nunuli—made rapid headway.

Finally, they came to an area where wounded and dead lay on the floor. At that point, amid the groans of the injured and the dying, Modyun felt a plucking at one elbow from behind.

"Where are you going?" asked the Nunuli. The smooth face seemed somehow different, as if its color was not quite as bright a gray as it normally was. And all the little worms on the head, seemed to be coiled into tiny knots, and lay very flat against the head.

"I thought we might go and have a talk with the Gunyan leader of the forces that have come aboard."

The Nunuli said briskly, "Why don't I authorize you to do just that. It would be rather foolish if I, as the master of the ship, placed myself at their mercy."

"I doubt if there would be any problem," said Modyun. He was mildly surprised at the objection. "They'll probably be happy to learn that you are prepared to abandon the attack. You *are*, aren't you?"

"Oh, absolutely." The creature spoke sincerely. "In fact, if you can persuade them to let us have our ground forces back, tell them we'll leave at once."

8   113

"I'm greatly relieved to hear you say that," said Modyun. "But I believe it would be better if you said it."

The Nunuli was backing away. "I think I ought to be in the control room, marshalling our forces to defend the forward part of the ship in the event that the enemy launches their assault before you can speak to them. I seem to notice that no one is doing anything about that."

It was true. It occurred to Modyun that the bodies around them, dead as well as living, were persons who had somehow walked or staggered or crawled out of the carnage further to the rear. And the Gunyan forces were probably mobilizing in several of the large parks at this back end of the ship.

"Well," he admitted aloud, "what you say may be a good idea. There may be some fine timing here, and difficulty in communicating. In order to save lives, which"—he was remembering the total interest in life prolongation of his four friends when they had been sentenced to death—"I'm sure is uppermost in everybody's mind. I imagine," he addressed the alien, "this is also your concern."

The Nunuli seemed to have recovered his bright gray coloration. "As a matter of fact," he said, "I have a directive from the committee not to expose myself unnecessarily. In my zeal for peace I seem to have done just that. So I'd better leave quickly."

"I don't know about you and peace—" began Modyun. And stopped. He was addressing a rapidly retreating Nunuli who, after a few moments, whisked into a side corridor and was gone.

He resumed his walking. Though it wasn't needed—in such a confined area, his real defenses would be automatic—he indicated signal awareness out of curiosity. The first signal feedback came almost immediately. Its implication was that he was being watched through fairly sophisticated instruments that could build up images without direct viewing of the target.

Presently he perceived that doors were softly opening, and that he was already in Gunyan-controlled territory. A number of living beings—presumably, soldiers—stepped into the corridor out of rooms behind him; cut off his retreat.

Good, he thought. They've observed the purposeful pattern in my approach, I hope.

Abruptly, he felt an indication sensation in his brain. Something bright flashed past his shoulder.

Moydun did not turn but continued to walk at the same brisk

114

pace, taking care only not to trip over the dead bodies. Another bright flash whisked past his head, and then another. In his brain, the indication was a steady flow. But—he noticed—it was of a minimum nature. Protective, not resistant.

The creatures were not aiming directly at him. He surmised that they were testing his determination to continue on his present course.

As suddenly as it had started, the energy firing ceased. Moments after that, as he approached a cross corridor, half a dozen beings walked out from either side, and blocked his path.

Modyun stopped. He presumed he would now discover exactly what was the price of further progress.

The beings who confronted him were rugged types, square-built. They had heads and bodies and arms, but it was as if a roughly human shape slightly under six feet high had been cut out of marble.

Man is fashioned of soft clay; Gunyans from a hard, browny, seamy marble, thought Modyun.

One of the six creatures, who barred his way, gestured at him. It was an imperative motion. It seemed to command him to something. Having made the gesture, the Gunyan uttered a sharp sound. Immediately, he and his five companions divided into groups of three. One group took up position to his left and the other to his right. Modyun thought he got the idea. And, in fact, when he walked forward again, the two groups walked with him.

He was being escorted. Where? He hoped it was to a command post.

Suddenly, the individual who had already shown that he had some authority, detached himself from his unit of three, and ran awkwardly ahead to where several Gunyans stood at attention in front of an open door. He uttered sounds at these, and then, turning, with his deep-set eyes fixed on Modyun's peaceful ones, pointed at the open door.

Again, Modyun thought he understood. So he walked through the doorway.

He found that he had entered a huge auditorium—a theater, it looked like. It had a stage, and three tiers of seats for an audience of at least six thousand, with a small second gallery perched way up near the ceiling capable of holding a few hundred more.

Several Gunyans, presumably soldiers—for they held what seemed to be metal rods—peered down alertly at the scene below from this high vantage point. All the rest of the occupants of the auditorium were on the large stage. To the rear of the stage, about a hundred Gunyans were lined up in three ranks. They were standing, and they also carried metal rods. In front of these sat a second group. Of this seated group, there were at least three dozen. Standing, and apparently lecturing to those who were sitting, was an individual who looked no different from any of the others.

All hundred and thirty plus Gunyans seemed to be peering at a screen which had been erected at the front of the stage. But what was on the screen was not visible from where Modyun had paused just inside the door.

XXV

THE PATTERN of the drama on the stage changed suddenly, as the beings became aware of Modyun.

The individual, who had been addressing the others, ceased doing so. He walked in heavy fashion several steps closer to the edge of the stage near Modyun, and spoke in a rumbling voice. The words were directed to the human being's escort; since they were heard by so many, it was not a discourtesy to listen. So Modyun indicated thought—and the meaning of the words came through in the rough fashion of such translations:

"Bring that pig before me!"

The beast, the name of which matched the concept of an unmodified earth swine wallowing in some kind of filth, looked more like a small, horned cow in the picture that Modyun perceived from the other's brain.

He smiled in a pained way at the idea of such an inapplicable comparison. So he spoke and indicated thought at the same time:

"I have come here of my own free will. If you wish me to walk up onto the stage, I'll be glad to do so."

"Oh—you speak our language!" The Gunyan commander was startled. "Well, I'm glad we have someone to talk to."

Modyun decided it would be too complex to explain the nature of the thought indication that, when utilized in conjunction with the spoken word, gave the impression that one was hearing the language itself. What was especially good about the method was that it limited invasion of the other person's thoughts to the meaning of the words uttered.

By the time he had these awarenesses, he was walking rapidly forward. The six members of his escort ran beside him in their awkward fashion, and managed to keep abreast of him. There were broad steps leading up to the stage from the wings. As Modyun mounted these, he saw for the first time what was on the large screen at the front of the stage: a brilliant view of the land below, of the portion of the Gunyan planet apparently

117

directly under the earth ship. No one interfered with him, as he strode across the stage to where he could see the scene from a front position.

It was day below. Clear, bright, everything in sharp relief, seemingly only about half a mile down. Off to one side, a river wound through a forest, breaking out onto an immense plain immediately under the ship. On this plain, occupying a portion of both side of the river, the Earth army was—not entrenched; that would have been the wrong view of its desperate predicament. But there it was, grounded.

There were Gunyan armies to the north, east, south, and west. They pressed in upon the Earth forces, compressed them into an area about two miles square. Which was a pretty small space for a quarter of a million individuals and their equipment.

Between these intensely held-in armies and the Gunyan forces, a battle was taking place. Huge bursts of bright, colored fire kept falling among the Earth animals, and brilliant flame spots erupted in a continuous spraying of fire among the distant Gunyan armies.

It all looked very severe and deadly in the quick view that Modyun allowed himself before he turned abruptly from the screen. "We must stop that battle as soon as possible. There is no further necessity for either the armies of Gunya or of Earth to suffer additional casualties."

"Who are you?" The Gunyan commander spoke curtly.

"My name is Modyun. And your name?"

"I am a general of the Gerd. Doer is my name."

"General Doer, I represent the Nunuli Master of this Earth ship. Let us stop the carnage."

There was a long pause. Then, grimly, the reply: "The battle will be stopped only with the total annihilation or total surrender of the invading force."

Modyun sighed as he had seen Ichdozh do, by opening his mouth and exhaling. What he finally said was, "That is an unnecessary solution. After all, we both know the only people being hurt are dupes. Naturally, the leaders will neither surrender nor expose themselves to annihilation. So your alternatives are unrealistic."

"The punishment must fit the crime." Savagely. "They are members of an invading, aggressive force, and it was their intention to take over Gunya."

118

"Dupes have no meaningful intentions," said Modyun. "Besides, whatever the individual responsibility, the conditions have changed. They are now willing to withdraw from this planet and this attack, if your bridgehead group will get off the ship and we are allowed to reembark our men."

The thought-form of the creature facing him showed the same grim attitude. "War, once engaged in," he said, "is not that easy to disengage from. We require the total surrender of this ship and of the planet—Earth, did you call it?—which dared to send forces to invade Gunya."

Modyun shook his head. "These are old-fashioned thoughts," he said. "War is not fixed one way or another. It's just something that should never start in the first place. But, if started, should be ended as soon as possible. It is your good fortune that the attack has failed. The sooner you think of it from that point of view, the sooner you'll see that nothing is to be gained by your adamant answer. End this war while my group feels defeated. It is possible they may think of something or get charged up with the same emotion that you have, and then they won't give up."

There was a long pause. General Doer stood and stared at him from those deep-set eyes. He seemed to be grappling with the meaning of what the human being had said. Finally: "Are we discussing the same subject?" he asked.

Modyun was surprised. He had stated his position, it seemed to him, with his usual adherence to essentials. Yet in dealing with irrational people he had already discovered that they tended to distort basic truth. So he said now, spelling it out, "My subject is the withdrawal of your forces from this ship and the peaceful embarkation of our ground troops. In exchange, the Nunuli Master agrees to abandon his aggressive plan against Gunya."

"Oh!" said the other, sarcastically, "I couldn't be sure. My impression was that the enemy had sent an insane person as a negotiator."

"Sanity is, of course, a relative matter—" Modyun began.

He was cut off harshly, "Your armies and your ship are totally at our mercy. Yet you come here and act as if it's the other way around. Who the hell are you? And what is all this gobbledy-gook?"

Those were not the exact words, naturally, but that was a fair interpretation of what was a rough-worded colloquial speech.

"I'm a passenger," Modyun said. "Well, that is—" He stopped, wondering if he could define the position of the last human being of Earth. His role on the ship: an unwelcome guest, who was not considered dangerous, but who could not be removed. He supposed what he was trying to do was to find Soodleel and have a conversation with a member of the committee. He finished his statement, bearing those vague purposes in mind, "I'm not involved in all this." He waved at the Gunyan soldiers, and extended his gesture to take in the huge viewplate. "But I was willing to talk to you. However, if your attitude is what you say, then no further conversation is necessary. If you cannot be reasoned with—and evidently you cannot be—I'll return to my part of the ship."

"That," said the creature in front of him significantly, "is not true. You're not going anywhere. On Gunya, we send the heads of unsuccessful negotiators back to their superiors."

A sound rumbled from the other beings on the stage. It was—Modyun analyzed—Gunyan satirical laughter.

He shook his head chidingly. "I should warn you that this body of mine does not tolerate personal threats. It's been quite a lesson to me to discover that the ancient human beings were actually incapable of living by a passive philosophy. I've been trying to analyze how I can bypass its automatic overwhelm indications, and so my solution in a crisis like this would be to make a deliberate, mild violation of your mental privacy. I apologize in advance, and in fact before I do so I call your attention to the possibility that I may be the only one aboard that can, uh, speak your language. Are you sure you should threaten an interpreter who—"

He stopped.

Because at that exact instant he experienced a power warmth in one of his indication centers. He turned a little, and looked in the direction from which the warmth derived. As he did so, the lights of the auditorium started to flicker.

He had time to think: For God's sake, *that* . . . in an otherwise backward culture like the Gunyan. And then he thought more fleetingly that their knowledge of the phenomenon apparently didn't include the realization that one didn't use it near a planetary body.

No further critical thought was possible.

He was involved with everything his brain could muster split-instant by instant.

XXVI

MODYUN DID not consider what he did next as the opening moves of a battle. Had such a consideration even crossed his mind, he might have hesitated—and at those superspeeds that could have been fatal. To him, what happened was an energy thing. And he was simply, and instantly—and quite enormously—interested in observing a phenomenon of space that he had never seen but had heard of.

In that first semimoment, his brain had indicated awareness of black-hole manifestation. The actual measurement that came through to him was eight kilometers.

Pretty small.

Originally a blue sun, he noted. After nuclear burning up of its hydrogen, it had expanded into a red giant and rapidly—unusually rapidly—exhausted its helium, carbon, oxygen, silicon, and so on up to a moment (in terms of stellar time) of stability as iron. But the iron also was exhausted, and what had been a great star sought and found another brief stability as a white dwarf.

The next collapse was to the fabulous matter insanity of neutron star. But equilibrium as a mass of even moonlet size had not been possible for this unusual structure. It became a singularity, eight kilometers in diameter.

A gravitational hole.

Modyun thought, amazed: These Gunyans must have such a singularity in nearby space. So they've learned some of its laws, and are about to defeat the committee. Seemed incredible. Hard to grasp that they actually might have such an advanced technology. But—no question, they were tapping its gravitation on a controlled basis.

That's why the landing craft had become immobilized, impossible to get off the ground. Red giant sun (equivalent) level gravitation held them immovable.

About ten seconds went by as he had these thoughts. Which was a long time in the microscopic universe of a black-hole.

He could feel the ship shuddering under him as its computers tried to adjust to the moment by moment shift in gravitational (and magnetic) interflow. Tried to interrelate with a singularity. With matter and energy madness. Impossible, of course.

In those ten seconds, the balancing power of the gigantic machinery of the ship was impelled through all its potential gravity-moments. It failed to locate a point of equilibrium.

At once the great vessel began to fall.

Now, gravitation, Modyun reminded himself, is not a force. In a way it was not even a field in the ordinary magnetic meaning of such a term. It was *easier* for two bodies in space to have a relation-toward than a relation-away. That was the only reason that so huge a vessel could come near a planet's surface. Yes, it was easier to have a relation-toward—but such a relation didn't have to exist. What the ship's "motors" did was to set up a field whereby every particle in its bulk *ignored* the presence of a planetary body.

The force was controllable, adjustable to *any* percentage of the whole. And so this vessel had been maneuvered into gravitational equilibrium about half a mile above the ground of Gunya.

The use of black-hole gravitation upset that balance.

But still the ship fell only as an object free falls through an atmosphere. On Earth, sixteen feet the first second, thirty-two the second; on Gunya about the same. On such fine matters, the difference between the two planets, measured in inches or centimeters per second per second, came to—a few.

No indication system existed that could deal with such colossal forces directly.

Somebody is doing this, Modyun thought. And he or they could be contacted.

But still he did not think of it as a battle. He simply put into effect his previous decision to obtain information from General Doer. His indication elicited confusion. Fear. The entire brain and body of the Gunyan reflected conviction of imminent disaster.

"All right, all right," the Gunyan leader yelled in the darkness, "we'll get off. But for God's sake don't crash the ship!"

He didn't know!

Startled, Modyun took the next step: indicated awareness of the surrounding space.

And saw a face—

Not human. Not Gunyan. Not Nunuli.

Intent face. A slightly triangular head. Two eyes, almost blood red in color, narrowed. Those slitted eyes seemed to stare straight into Modyun's. But for a tiny accretion of time, that was only true in a gross physical meaning. During that infinitesimal period, the mind behind the eyes was not aware that there was an observer.

During that period, Modyun indicated thought, and said, "Who are you? Why are you doing this?"

The automatic answer began, "I am the committee member—the special agent—who destroyed the human beings behind the barrier. And now, by another method of equal power, the knowledge of which is also exclusively reserved for committee members, I—"

At that split-instant, the being became aware of Modyun. The automatic flow of his thought ceased.

Modyun was astounded by the cutoff.

In the darkness of the theater around him, there was a confusion of Gunyan scrambling and Gunyan incoherent throaty sounds. Beneath him, the ship was falling. His stomach had the sensation that comes with a too-rapid descent of an elevator.

For Modyun, these were background events. In that moment, he felt such a craving for information that he indicated total enforced response from the distant committee member—without noticing what a complete violation it was of the alien being's mental privacy.

As the indication reached its peak power, the strange, intent face, instead of growing clearer—faded. In its place, as if seen in a clear but troubled pool, was the head and shoulders of somebody with golden hair. The vision shimmered, and then steadied, and became—

Soodleel.

Modyun had an impression of a vast distance between the human woman and himself. But her blue eyes gazed directly into his as if they were only inches away. And her thought came to his thought indication receivers, sharp, unmistakable, but strangely sad. *Modyun, I need your help. I'm trapped by a Zouvgite, a committee member—*

The communication ended. The image of her in that remote space remained intensely visible, but if she was still indicating thought it was not coming through. To Modyun, there came the

123

memory of what the Nunuli had told him about the Zouvg method of one-directional mind control.

It's true!

Incredibly, a single Zouvgite, presumably without assistance, was capable of such an intensity of one-way mental flow that . . . he was resisting—delaying the indication system.

XXVII

MODYUN MADE what was, for him, an odd analysis: he found himself believing that the abrupt substitution of the image of Soodleel for that of a committee member was connected. The substitution was a scheme. An enforced cause-and-effect relationship, which he could be aware of because he had gradually had to adjust his brain to the distorted purposes of beings with ulterior motives.

All around him, as he had these awarenesses, was the intense darkness of a large auditorium in what Modyun guessed was now a completely unlighted ship. Somehow, as happens with great bodies falling through air, the vessel had tilted. It was as if the huge mass of atmosphere that was being compressed aside by the falling monster, and shifting at gale velocities over the square miles of the craft's undersurface, had found extrusions and protuberances that caused unbalances in the rate of fall of different sections. The floor as beginning to slant forward. Modyun had to stand like a man on a slope with one leg slightly bent, the other stiff, to brace him.

Standing there somewhat awkwardly, he realized: Soodleel's predicament is being brought to my attention at this moment to keep me occupied while the ship falls the rest of the way to the ground.

Which it would do now in a few dozen seconds.

Pretty tricky stuff—

His body felt warm, and involved. His face was almost hot, his eyes tensed and burning; and his teeth were clamped hard together. He thought: The committee member is actually stil l standing there—hiding behind Soodleel's image.

Only one thing to do. He indicated for total truth.

It should again have been instantaneous but several seconds went by. And, during that whole time, the force of the indication continued to interact with the committee member and the image he was trying to maintain.

Abruptly Soodleel's face grew misty. Again, the sense of distance—Modyun had the feeling that she was receding even farther.

She was gone. Where she had been with her strange little request for help was—

Blankness.

In the great theater auditorium, the lights flickered and came back on. Simultaneously, there was the empty stomach and overall body effect of a slowing down elevator. The stop was like jumping ten or fifteen feet, and ploughing to rest in a mud bank. Modyun lost his breath. His knees buckled, and he fell awkwardly to the floor.

The "elevator" started up. The speed had a G-plus impact and held him pressed down to the floor. As he lay there, momentarily helpless, he realized what had happened. In breaking away from Modyun's indication, the committee member had had to withdraw. Abandon what he was doing. Cut off the black-hole.

So, several things were happening.

Automatically, the great vessel's lift system adjusted back to its preset relation with the planet below. The strain was terrific. The ship's structure howled as every molecule was modified, by theory, equally; but in fact with tiny variations because different elements were involved. Floors whined, walls shuddered, everything bent and twisted a little from those variations.

Unfortunately, what was happening was minor compared to the real threat. A singularity had been brought into close proximity of a planet. Somewhere, that awesome thing was seeking to recover *its* balance. When those readjustments finally inverted upon the macrocosm, there would be inconceivably massive enturbulation.

As soon as he was able, Modyun climbed to his feet. And saw that General Doer was likewise regaining his equilibrium. Pretty quick. Pretty brave. But the Gunyan's first words were stupid. The alien said, "I knew you wouldn't crash your ship on your own army below."

It was not the moment to deal with a field commander's miscomprehension. Modyun said, "Put me in contact with your top leader." He indicated instant compliance.

Less than half a minute later, he was summarizing for another rugged-faced Gunyan—whose image flashed abruptly onto the screen—the story of the Zouvgites, the galactic conquest intentions of the committee, and at least a preliminary attempt to describe the gravitational whirlpool that was a black hole.

His ending advice was: "Broadcast worldwide warnings. Tell your people to get under a solidly fastened object, like the floor of a house that has a concrete foundation embedded in the soil. Under that floor, fasten mattresses or anything soft, so that when the sudden, crushing upward pull of gravitation comes, people will fall up onto the mattresses. Since time in a black-hole is dead slow, the first reaction will probably not come for several hours."

He completed his communication with a total compliance indication.

Would any protective method work? Modyun wasn't sure. He actually foresaw the possibility that solid chunks of Gunya would fly off into space.

In fact, the outlook for the Gunyans was so deadly that he said to General Doer, "I think your troops should remain aboard, and, if you can, get an equal number of Gunyan females in here. But right now, escort me out of your territory to where I can contact the ship's control room. I sensed earlier that they were disconnecting from this part of the vessel."

As it turned out, he didn't wait to get to a communicator. Instead, as he walked, he indicated awareness, and thus located the Nunuli.

Indicated thought. And, again, compliance.

. . . Get the troops aboard. Go up slowly, and maintain a position about a hundred miles above the army. Issue a shipwide warning that we may be subjected to variant upward gravitational pull. Everyone, sleep strapped in.

Which was about as much as he could do.

Modyun returned to his cabin. And it was there that the guilt hit him.

Have I ever been violating the mental privacy of other people! He slept uneasily, with that burden on his conscience.

XXVIII

HE AWAKENED to awareness of a muffled sound—and to a startled thought. The sound came through the walls of his cabin from the corridor outside. The thought was: When I located the Nunuli to give him those orders, where was he?

It had not been in a normal place, as he recalled it. As usual, of course, he had been intent on not prying into another person's activities any more than he absolutely had to for his purposes at the time.

But I've got to remember that all that (what happened) was for me.

It was Modyun, the Earthman, that these Zouvgites were trying to destroy. He was out of bed by the time that concept completed. He had to assume that another death plan was already going forward. By the time he had considered some of the meaning of *that* realization, he was fully dressed.

He opened the door.

Bedlam greeted him.

At least, that was the initial impact upon his senses. The sound of the bedlam was a continuous roar of voices and a continuous shuffle of feet.

The sight? The hallway was packed with grimy animal-men, carrying packsacks and electric rifles.

There was an odor of (presumably) Gunyan mud intermixed with the scent of un-Earthly plant life. Each individual had apparently spent part of his time lying on grass, on leaves, and brush, and had ground the stuff into his clothing; and it smelled.

As he gazed on that living river of returned soldiers, Modyun was aware of a feeling of content welling up from his body: Maybe all this interference isn't really that bad. That was the message.

But he was also remembering his previous venture along this hallway: how difficult it had been for him and the Nunuli to make headway, earlier, against a similar stream of animal people. Do I really want to get involved in all that again? Thousands of years of human noninvolvement told him no. But there was inside him a new, intense feeling; a peculiar, heated determination that derived from a conviction that he should at least have a discussion with the committee before he decided about his own future. *That* feeling urged him forward.

He maneuvered himself over to the first rows of elevators and was swept into a packed machine going up. He got off at the very top, by which time only a gold-braided hyena officer (whom he had never seen before) and he were left.

Modyun was slightly surprised when the other man walked across the foyer to the same second-row elevator as he. In fact, it seemed so coincidental that he turned and looked at the hyena officer—and for the first time saw that his companion's uniform was spotless. Obviously, he was not one who had been down in the dirt of Gunya.

The two stood silently in front of the elevator door. But it was not until the door finally glided open that the officer spoke. He had evidently been observing Modyun, and thinking. "Are you sure you should be going up here?" he asked. "It's a restricted area."

"Oh, yes," said Modyun. He spoke casually, because he had made up his mind; and of course opposition at this stage meant nothing.

"I would have sworn," said the hyena-man, "that no apes are allowed in this section."

"I am," said Modyun. He spoke calmly, and immediately afterwards stepped inside the elevator. He was conscious of the officer following him, and aware that the other was eyeing him doubtfully. As the machine got under way, the hyena-man stood sort of stiffly, visibly in conflict. Modyun, who had been preoccupied with his own intention—which was simply to locate the Nunuli and talk to him—grew more alert to the small crisis that was developing beside him. Perhaps a knowledgeable remark would head it off. He said courteously, "I'm going to have a talk with the Nunuli Master."

He was watching the other's somewhat brownish tanned face closely as he spoke. And there was no question: this was one of the hierarchy. He knew of the Nunuli. The officer said in a surprised tone, "Then you must be scheduled to go along."

Modyun's eyes did not so much as flicker. "Oh, yes," he said. And indicated for additional information, saying, "When do we leave?"

"About a dozen more to come," was the reply. The hyena-man added, not noticing how totally he was revealing the secret, which, surely, he must have been told not to discuss with anyone. "The scientists are still setting up the hydrogen bomb, which is to be exploded by remote after we takeoff. They have still to come aboard."

Modyun had almost missed it—almost gone to bed for the night. Almost—but not quite. Okay, he thought gloomily, so I've been that close to ultimate foolishness. That close to letting a million people be blown up by a group which was willing to sacrifice so many individuals in order to exterminate one human being. In a way of course it didn't matter. They were all mortal, and would eventually die anyway. But what bothered him—he realized—was a kind of unfair advantage the committee was taking of its superior knowledge and science. Misuse of power— *really*. He could feel all through his body his adverse reaction to that unfairness.

This, he thought, is my preprograming.

The elevator was coming to a stop, and he had no time to consider it further. The door opened; and there, only yards away, was what was unmistakably the airlock of a large vessel, which was poised for upward launching.

That was where he had vaguely noticed the Nunuli to be at the time of his previous indication.

The vessel, he saw, was mostly hidden behind the launching walls, but he could see the contours of a curving shape where the corridor wall bulged to fit. The airlock doors were open; and the two of them entered side by side. The first person Modyun saw, as he stepped through the second door, was the Nunuli Master.

The alien had his back to the door, and he was saying something about the necessity for a quick departure. His remark elicited a courteous response from half a dozen hyena engineers. They all bowed. One, acting as spokesman, said, "We're ready for takeoff, sir. Close the doors, flip three switches, and we're gone."

"Take your stations, then!" the Nunuli commanded. "I'll wait right here personally for the last arrivals and—" He had been turning away as he spoke. His voice ceased because at that instant he saw Modyun.

130

There was a long moment of awkward silence. Then Modyun said gently, "As I see it, I should just indicate no further plots against me, including this one; and of course issue no additional flight orders until we have passed through the black-hole."

"Until we have *what?*" said the other.

"I really don't think I'll have time to explain," said Modyun. "But it's interesting to me that you were kept unaware. They were willing to sacrifice you, also, weren't they? The very fact that you came to my cabin for help proved you didn't know what was about to happen."

He was turning away, intending to leave, when the Nunuli said urgently, "Wait!"

Modyun stopped, politely.

The alien continued, "I should perhaps tell you that I have been advised that, in view of this new development, a member of the committee is now willing to explain to you the committee's long-term program."

Modyun was struck by the wording. "In view of what new development?" he asked.

The alien seemed surprised. "Your action in coming here to this escape ship, thus nullifying the final logical solution, which—it was hoped—would resolve the problem of the last human male once and for all."

Modyun was still striving to grasp some basic meanings. "Let me understand this. A member of the committee is now willing *personally* to talk to me?"

"Yes."

Modyun stood there, a little blank, a little shaken. But conscious also of a pleasantly warm feeling that was manifesting in a nerve center in the lower middle of his body. Victory? It felt like it. And it felt good. I will see Soodleel again . . . The thought brought his first real awareness that her departure had disturbed him very much. He thought: Maybe one of these hours, I can even let down the sensory blocks that I put up when I came from behind the barier.

That was something Soodleel had failed to do. And so she had been impelled, in the restless need for motion of the innumerable motor cells of a human brain, to take a walk that very first afternoon. As a result, somewhere in the far distance of the galaxy—it had felt far indeed—she was lost and trapped. A little difficult

131

to know how they could have her trapped, and leave her alive—but her appeal for help had implied both conditions.

Remembering that, Modyun thought of all the precautions he would have to take, to ensure that the meeting with the Zouvg was not itself another conspiracy against him; and he said, "When do we leave? I'm ready any time."

"Are you out of your mind!" Having spoken, the alien must have realized the cause of Modyun's misconception. He went on, "What I meant was, a committee member will talk to you if you ever find where he is." He was suddenly tolerant. "The big concession here is that you now have an advance agreement that a committee member is willing to talk to you."

Modyun waited courteously for the other to finish, then he said, "I took that for granted. Finding him is no real problem as I see it. I can think of three separate methods, because location in space is one of my indication abilities. As you may know—"

He stopped. Turned his head slightly. Stood there, this giant of man slightly over eight feet tall with a head that was large in proportion. Handsome, intent face pointed. Eyes narrowed slightly. "It's starting," he said. "You'll be floating soon. Take your pad with you, and lie on the ceiling when the time comes."

As he turned once more to the door, he was again stopped by the Nunuli's voice, "When *what* time comes?" the creature asked in an alarmed tone. "*What's starting?*"

"We're entering the black-hole," said Modyun. "I figured it would be the most direct route. Remember what I told you: Issue a general warning that this ship may be subject to cross-gravitational pressures throughout the night."

"B-but—why?"

"I," said Modyun, "believe that such a perfect little black-hole —only eight kilometers—would never be allowed far from some easy point of control and ownership."

The implications of that must have penetrated, for the Nunuli's eyes misted, showing suddenly almost blue. "Oh, my God!" he said in animal vernacular.

"So," concluded the human being, "when the fireworks are over, we'll find that we have been drawn to the vicinity of the planet of Zouvg . . . is my prediction. In either slightly less than or more than one Earth day," he concluded. "Good night, sir."

He hurried out.

XXIX

MODYUN ARRIVED at his cabin, breathless, and thought: Now that the Nunuli cannot act against me, I'll have to watch for some kind of direct attack from the committee itself.

He undressed, went to bed, strapped himself in—and slept.

. . . and awakened with the feel of the belts tugging at his body. He estimated three G's.

He was uneasy, but . . . philosophical. By theory, the push-pull inside a singularity could be thousands of gravities. Yet the ship's engines were designed to adjust to extreme attraction situations. This, added to their enormous speed potentialities, made possible shifts in position forward and sideways. Up, down, left, right. And always the built-in purpose would seek a least-stress location . . . No use fretting about. Trust—

Altogether there were four peak gravity moments. Each time Modyun lay in the dark—or rather floated—and let himself be aware of the colossal speed, first of acceleration, and then of deceleration, as the giant vessel passed through the equivalent distance of scores of light-centuries.

And passed through the black-hole.

At the instant of emergence, he was asleep. And in his mind was a mental picture of Soodleel without clothes on, as he had seen her that first passionless afternoon. Somehow, in the sleep vision, the—memory—stirred a previously unrealized feeling in him. And he was about to examine what that feeling might be when he had the shocked realization that he, a human being, was actually experiencing sleep-time visual feedback.

Modyun awakened, astonished. A dream! He? But animals dreamed to solve problems, and to throw off the conflicts of the previous day from the perceiving, registering senses.

I'm sinking . . . That was the disturbed thought. Dreaming was a first symptom that the daytime conscious mind was not coping.

He paid no attention at first to the content of the dream. It was the *act* of dreaming that dismayed him. Yet presently he became aware that the dream had brought about the genital rigidity which he had seen previously only in male animals.

I'll be darned. So that's how you do that?

Enormously interested, he got up and studied the phenomenon in the bathroom mirror. But the condition was apparently not capable of enduring such close examination. Thus scrutinized, there was a swift deterioration.

But he was cheerful as he dressed. He replayed the dream mentally several times, strictly for what—he realized—was its erotic content. He was in the act of combing his hair, when it belatedly occurred to him that an unusual event like a dream just might have another significance.

Part of a new attack?

Perhaps while his brain was absorbed with its first passion, an action had taken place which he was not supposed to notice. Uneasily, he indicated awareness.

But the ship was peacefully coasting through normal space heading toward a nearby sun system. And in his mental energy field, there was only one dark area: the Nunuli. Even that wasn't as dark as it had been.

If anything happened, thought Modyun unhappily, it's done. And it's not a big enough event to leave an after-trail.

Which, of course, would be the ideal attack against such as he.

He finished dressing, and he was still considering the possible nature of an attack, when the doorbell buzzed. Modyun had an instant intuition, and started to the door. Almost at once, he experienced a cautioning thought—and he stopped: It's time I cease being pure, and realize that their plotting has been against one person—myself. Seemed incredible, yet there was no question. Beginning with the first two attacks by hyena-men, and culminating in the colossal phenomenon of the singularity, the human race as personified by one male, was the target.

They initiated that dream about the nature of sexual arousal. Evidently, they needed something that would totally absorb his attention while they mounted a final attack. Since he had made it impossible for the Nunuli Master of the ship to do anything against him . . . "they," of course, would be a member of the committee.

Still difficult to grasp that a Zouvgite was taking a personal interest in the fate of one man from one small planet. But there was no question. The venomous red-eyed creature, so briefly

134

contacted at the height of the black-hole attack, had admitted his identity. Equally significant, they had been willing for their Nunuli servant to go down with the ship—had given him no advance warning of the attack. Fantastic reality, but true.

Whatever it is, I'm as ready as I'll ever be. Standing there, he set up all levels of indication so that if one were triggered all would come on.

With that reassurance, he walked to the door, and opened it. There, as he had intuited, stood all four of his animal friends, grinning sheepishly.

"Hey!" said Modyun, "come on in."

By the time he spoke those words, he was already fighting for his life.

XXX

THERE WAS a bright flash from the barrel of a gun. The charge coruscated like a bolt of lightning along the corridor, making a hideous crackling roar. It grounded, of course, after traveling only a few dozen feet.

"Ichdozh," said Roozb irritably, "watch what you're doing." He turned to Modyun. "Hi," he said, grinning.

It was all over as quickly as that. An attempt to burn out his brain. And, when that failed, the instant destruction of the mechanism used.

Now, he would not be able to analyze what was their method of matching the human indication system. But how desperately determined they must be to have taken the chance of revealing to him that they had such a method.

Modyun had no time to think about it immediately. Because, as Dooldn entered, he found himself grabbed, and hugged, and passed on to each of the animal-men in turn.

"Boy, are we ever glad to see you!"

His hand was shaken furiously. Narrl's affectionate arm encircled his neck and shoulder, and then shoved him against the powerful chest of Roozb, who gave him a squeeze that almost took his breath away.

"Hey!" Modyun managed to say, "fellows, you made it!"

They were, he learned presently, fairly well recovered from their experience. But the four were still excited.

"Boy!" said the bear-man, shaking his head, "that place down there is an unmodified rattlesnake nest. We've taken on more than we can handle. The sooner we're away from this planet, the better I'll like it." He added, "We managed to disengage, and get our troops back aboard, but—" He paused, looking grim.

The huge ship was already far away indeed from Gunya, but Modyun presumably wouldn't know any more about that than they did. "The place down there" now was another, far more interesting place. So he said nothing.

Beside Modyun, the fox-man made an inarticulate sound as the bear-man finished speaking. The human glanced at the other. "What's the matter, Narrl?"

A tear rolled down the fox-man's cheek. "Funny, I never thought of this as a voyage of conquest. Suppose we did conquer these—whatchamecallems? What would we do with them?"

"It's these damned hyena-men," Ichdozh grunted. "It's like Modyun said. They're a bunch of usurpers with vicious ideas."

Listening to them, Modyun began to feel quite a bit better. They were—true—blaming the hyena-men, who were only slightly less dupes than they were; and of course they would never attack Gunya again. But the vehemence of their protest held a promise that perhaps others of the animal people aboard might be as easily stirred to resistance.

It was a vagrant thought only; not really a serious purpose. Yet it had the look of a solution of sorts—as if a man *could* take back control of the animal people of Earth.

It was, he realized, too soon for that kind of meaning. Aloud, he said heartily, "Well, you four won't be going down again. It's somebody else's turn next time, eh?"

"Then why were we called out this morning and told to carry our electric rifles until further notice?" Dooldn complained.

So that was how it was done.

"Any trouble with your guns?" Modyun asked casually.

Roozb did a disgusted gesture with his shoulder. "A hyena officer spotted a problem in Ichdohz's rifle, and that held us up coming over here whilst it was fixed. But maybe—hey!" His large, brown, innocent eyes widened. "Maybe it still isn't properly fixed. Maybe that's why it discharged here at the door. What do you think, Ichdohz?"

The hippopotamous-man acknowledged that maybe that was the explanation. Whereupon, Modyun, feeling greatly enlightened by the simplicity of the conspiracy (whereby presumably a committee member had bypassed the Nunuli, and directly influenced a hyena-man), said, "Well, after all, asking you to keep your rifle with you is only a natural precaution. Still doesn't mean you're scheduled for more action."

It was a possibility which apparently had not occurred to them. They brightened at once, and were soon gaily reporting some of their grim experiences on Gunya. Now that it was over, their laughter came shrilly, as they relieved themselves by recounting and laughing of and at and about the hideously dangerous moments.

Presently it seemed to Modyun that enough time had gone by. All the while they talked, he had been thinking.

And he had made up his mind.

He climbed to his feet. It was quite a moment, then, for him as he walked off to one side. Turning, he faced the four, raised one hand to get their attention and, when he had it, said, "Fellows, I have something important to tell you."

Standing there, he told them in simple words who he was, what he had done so far, and the problem that remained. After he had finished there was a long silence. Finally, Roozb got up and came over and silently shook his hand. It was the signal for the others to do the same.

But they sat down again, and their bright eyes fixed on him, waiting for what was next. But it was Roozb who said soberly, "So here you are, with your indication ability capable of being cancelled out."

Modyun had to admit that that was probably the truth. "There's only one thing about that I don't understand," he said. "Undoubtedly, what they've now shown they can do to me is what was also done to Soodleel. Yet they didn't kill her. Why not?"

Narrl said gloomily, "They saved her to use against you like you described. This Zouvg held her sort of in front of him, so you couldn't hit him."

"But," argued Modyun, "if they could really control the indication method that completely, why bother with all this other stuff?"

Dooldn, who had not previously spoken, said suddenly, "I can't see any real problem for the future. You just stay far enough away from these Zouvgs and their tricky method of controlling your brain, and"—he waved a dismissing hand—"you've got the problem licked."

"Yeah, hey!" said Ichdohz.

Both Roozb and Narrl brightened. "Yeah, that's it," said the fox-man.

"Well-ll—" said Modyun in a temporizing tone.

The pause that followed was embarrassing for him. What they were suggesting, human beings did not do; not for an avoidance reason. A human being was—he took it for granted, he realized —a superior life-form.

His problem had never been: could he or did he dare? He not so much dared as failed to react with fear. If he avoided a situation, it was for a philosophical reason, and that didn't apply any longer. In *this* situation, he had made up his mind to talk to a committee member. He explained that decision unhappily.

"Somebody has to go in and find out what they're up to, and argue them out of it if they can't explain it properly. And frankly I don't see how they can. For example, they've got a million men from Earth out here on a mission of conquest."

Somebody should tell them how inconvenient such a program was to all the people involved, both those being attacked and those attacking; in some instances cutting short their lives; in others. "Like you," he said, "scrambling around in the Gunyan mud was no fun, was it?"

His four friends agreed.

"That's what I mean," said Modyun. "So what I want to do is make a landing near one of those buildings down there and go in and talk to a committee member."

"But he'll use that thingamajig on your indication ability with more power behind it," protested Narrl, "and he'll have you trapped."

Modyun made a dismissing gesture, as Narrl himself often did. "That's unimportant," he said.

"For Pete's sake—" It was Dooldn; explosively. "Are you nuts?" He turned to the others. "Fellows, these human beings are kind of soft in the brain."

It was the barrier-breaking reaction.

They had been awed. A Man. A descendant of their ancient creator! And so they had been subdued by an image of—to them —superhuman overtones. The jaguar-man's outburst freed them.

Roozb growled, "Listen, friend, your heart's in the right place, but you'll never get off Zouvg alive, with ideas like that."

"Look," Narrl spoke, "you've got all that scientific knowledge. Isn't there some way in which that tells you that the Zouvg are vulnerable?"

The fox-man's question startled Modyun. He said slowly, "As a matter of fact, if I had let my thought go in the direction of violence—the truth is, the committee doesn't know as much about either the Ylem or a singularity as people should do who make use of such things."

Dooldn jumped to his feet. "Never mind the intellectual stuff," he said. "You got a practical thought here that can be used?"

Modyun drew a deep breath. "The third law of motion," he said quietly, "operates in the Ylem as it does in ordinary space, with of course the difference that it's a maintaining wave."

"What does that mean?" That was Ichdohz, intense, leaning forward.

Dooldn said impatiently, "Action and reaction are equal and opposite." He snapped the explanation to the others. To Modyun, he said, "What's the point?"

"They shouldn't have exploded the human city behind the barrier, using Ylem power. The reaction is still going on somewhere." Modyun shook his head, chidingly. "If somebody ever finds out who knows about things like that—boy!"

"Could *you* be that somebody?" asked Roozb soberly.

"Me!" croaked Modyun.

And then he stood there, shocked. He had offered the information, not relating it to anybody or anything, least of all to himself. Now, he swallowed, and gulped, "Oh, I couldn't do that," he said. "That might end up in mass murder."

"Listen to this guy," snorted Ichdohz, disgusted.

Roozb climbed to his feet. He said, "We'll go down with you, and cover your approach with our electric rifles. We can argue later what you do."

"I thought," suggested Modyun, "we ought to put an army down there first. Not to shoot or anything like that. But, just, properly spread out, it would be hard to do anything against so many, particularly when they're right down there where the Zouvgs are."

"There," approved Dooldn, "is a good idea."

XXXI

THEY ATE breakfast. Then, accompanied by four somewhat-awed animal-men, Modyun led the way to the control room.

"Maybe they won't let us in," said Narrl doubtfully as they came to the entrance, which was a large door set well back in a spacious alcove. All around the entrance were different colored lights, and on the metal panel the words: AUTHORIZED PERSONNEL ONLY.

Indication power broke all those barriers. It also dismissed the men who were inside: hyena-men engineers and technicians. When the authorized personnel had departed, Modyun supervised the locking of all doors.

A few minutes after that, there was—

Zouvg!

Seen by way of the huge control room viewplate, it was a misty cloud-covered circle of brightness silhouetted against a black sky. As the magnification intensified, it showed a small city in the mountains—the city where the Zouvgites lived.

The committee!

At this distance, the tiny glow of the barrier that surrounded the city was not visible. But of course he understood barriers. So that didn't matter.

Nothing down there was easy to see. Cliffs and canyons and long shadows, and dark ravines; and only here and there the glint of a building. One perched high on a mountain peak, another at the bottom of a thousand-foot chasm.

As he watched that great scene, Modyun kept trembling. Not all in one place. Sometimes it was the foot; then a shoulder and arm . . . stomach and intestines; hips, lungs, and so on, cycling back and forth and around. The sensations shifted. They never ceased for an instant.

He had opened himself up to perception, and the resultant stimulation.

He could feel the pressure of the floor on his soles and heels, and the mildly sandpaperish smoothness of the inside cloth of his trousers on the skin of his legs. He breathed air that tickled—a little—all the way into and through his lungs. His face was warm with what was now a kind of perpetual emotion—of anger? He wasn't totally sure what feeling it was. Something that pushed at him.

Just to make sure what the feeling was *not*, he replayed his ancient credos: (1) People are what they are, and life is what it is —worthwhile. (2) If you trust them (or it), they (it) will trust you. (3) Give them love, and they'll respond with love. (4) Life is basically good. Never make a threatening move, and you'll be amazed at how peaceful things are. (5) Always turn the other cheek.

The meaning, he observed, simply ran its course through his head. It engaged no mental gears. It was a pleasant internal spinning of a set of thoughts that were undoubtedly true in a way but they were not literally true in an always fashion. Because, obviously, the Nunuli were not like that *now*. Nor the Zouvgites— at least not yet. Nor even some creatures of Earth. Maybe later, in the future, they would be. But not now.

He'd still have to be careful, of course. Still can't kill. Many other *can'ts*. These were things the Zouvgites would know about him.

He and his animal friends watched most of the day as a large army was landed down there in the mountains inside the barrier —without being resisted. So they're waiting for me, Modyun was pretty sure. He thrummed his feet in a rapid dance, which was an immediate expression of his pleasure.

I've really let the internal barriers down . . . What he felt, the body did immediately. It felt kind of good.

Later, as they sat down to eat, it was evident that the others had been watching him. For Dooldn said, "How smart are you, really? Where did you learn all those things like about the black-hole?"

"The indication methods, used as perception systems, are capable of directly perceiving all the phenomena of Nature," said Modyun. He added modestly, "It's nothing that I as an individual perfected. The Nunuli did it for us. I'm no smarter, no better, than anyone else—except that I have these special abilities."

Roozb, who had started to eat in his vigorous fashion, looked up. "That's gotta be the truth, fellows. Most of the things this guy has done since we've known him, have been pretty naive. Good-hearted, but not bright. Yet, no question—he's got some high-powered stuff cookin' in that noodle of his. Right, Modyun?"

Modyun was not happy with the bear-man's description of him. But he was anxious to have these animal friends of his accept him on a good personal basis; so now he nodded vigorously. "Right," he said.

"Nonetheless," he added after a moment, "But I'm not as naive as I used to be."

"That I've got to see," said Roozb. He glanced at Modyun. "No offense, my friend, I'm just facing the facts. For example"— he shook his head sadly—"imagine, you let the only human woman left in the world be filched from you by a simple plot. And you're not even thinking of doing anything about it."

"But I know where she is," defended Modyun.

"Where?" growled Roozb promptly.

"She's with that Zouvgite, of course."

The bear-man turned towards the others, and spread his hands helplessly. "You see what I mean," he said.

Narrl grinned across the table at Modyun. "I remember a female I used to be hot about. Before I was ready to throw her over, she ditched me for a smooth-talker. I knew where she was after that all right."

"And I," volunteered Ichdohz, "had a friend who decided to cross the ocean by boat. It sank in a storm, and he was drowned. I know where he is all right. What's left of him is down there in two miles of water."

"You see, Modyun," Roozb stared at the Man, "the way you talk, you don't seem to put two and two together."

Their friendly attack struck deep. He was a person who had come to realize that something was wrong . . . Man was defeated, he thought. Literally destroyed down to the last man and woman. And here I am still talking and acting like a winner.

Pretty ridiculous. And yet . . .

As they finally finished eating, Modyun said, "We'd better go to bed. Sometime during the night we will probably get the message that the pressure curve has gone up to the point where I can have that meeting down there. When that time comes, our bodies will feel better for having had some rest."

Dooldn glared at him suspiciously. "You've got some scheme going?" he demanded.

143

"I told you I'm not quite as naive as I used to be," protested Modyun. "That army down there has no commissaries. And they're not used to not eating."

The message came shortly after 3 A.M. shiptime.

XXXII

SEEN THROUGH the viewplates, their destination was not directly approachable—unless they landed on its roof. The building was perched tightly against a cliff that went up sheer behind it. In front was another cliff going down. It was not so sheer down, however, and not so far down—not more than two hundred feet.

There was a fairly level area below the building, but it was decorated with walks and fences that wound among shrubs and along a stream to the edge of a forest about two hundred yards from the building. To land anywhere on the level area would require the destruction of a walk or a fence; and that of course would be a very discourteous thing to do.

Modyun could make out a lacery of steps leading up the side of the cliff from the garden below—if garden was what it was—to the building above. So there seemed no question: this building and the grounds below were part of the same construction and landscaping complex.

The mountainside had many moving figures on it; no question, the animal army was on the way. But they were still off to the right, and with climbing to do. It would take perhaps an hour before they arrived, Modyun estimated anxiously. Possibly, he should delay his own start a little.

The nearest other open meadow was a fairly steep slope a quarter of a mile farther down the mountain. And it was there that Modyun brought down the lifeboat, and from there he led his four friends over the rough ground. A gentle breeze blew past them down hill. For someone as perceptive as Modyun, the air was noticeably oxygen-laden; according to the computer 35 percent of the atmosphere was oxygen. The exhilarated quintet was soon moving into and among the trees. Here they saw their first creature life.

What they saw seemed to be birds: small winged creatures that flitted through the upper tree branches. Modyun indicated both awareness and thought, and had tiny, fleeting impingements of

145

simple idea-forms. Pictures came of branches whizzing close by, and of sky views as seen through small, bright eyes.

But no schemes. The creatures were what they seemed to be. And that was the whole wilderness around them. Everything natural, even primitive.

Why, Modyun asked himself, puzzled, would anyone living in such an idyll feel it necessary to have communication and control with and over other planets. All they could ever hope to get from such dominance would be a peculiar awareness that they were creating effects in a far-off, unknown place, with it highly unlikely if not impossible that they would ever visit more than a few of the planets they controlled. So the entire satisfaction would derive from their own mental images of the event.

Why did they feel a need for such images?

The whole thing seemed very sad and futile.

Even as he had the thoughts, he and his friends arrived at the edge of the garden. Directly in front of them was the first of the whiteish walks: Modyun stepped gingerly onto it, stopped, and turned.

"I think you people should wait here," he said. "Sort of spread out among the brush." His voice, as he continued, sounded loud upon the silences around them. "My protective indications can reach this far; and so what I can do for myself, I can do for you also—at this distance. But if I don't come out before the soldiers arrive, go and get the lifeboat. You may have to rescue me."

The four were unusually subdued. Modyun glanced at their humanlike faces, and saw there awe, and a kind of pervasive uneasiness. It was Roozb who broke that thralldom. He said, in what was scarcely more than a hoarse whisper, "Boy, it gets you, doesn't it?"

But he shook hands with Modyun, and muttered, "Good luck, pal. Carry the ball over the goal line, hey."

The others came forward each in turn and shook hands also. Only Dooldn made a remark. "Take it easy, friend," he said. Modyun nodded, and faced forward.

From where he stood, everything seemed fabulously close. Seen from the ground, the gardenlike area was flatter than it had appeared from the sky. It was also now possible to see that what had seemed like dirt was apparently a kind of plastic on which a fine dust had gathered. The same dust was on the walks, but they were a different color. There were several cut, ornamental bridges

146

over the stream; what the ornament signified, if anything, was not obvious.

The Earthman moved forward without looking back, and soon crossed one of the bridges. From a distance, it like the others had seemed fragile; yet to his feet it was as solid as steel. A minute after that, he was climbing a staircase that led up toward the castlelike structure above.

He arrived at the top somewhat breathless, and saw that there was a dust-covered walkway to a transparent, glass-clear door less than two dozen feet from the cliff's edge.

Before proceeding, Modyun now for the first time turned and looked back—looked down at the figures of his friends. They were all still there, looking up at him.

He waved. They waved back.

That was all, except—there was a tear in one eye as he turned away. When you've got a body, he thought, you can really get attached to people.

It was obviously not the moment for such feelings. So he walked to the door, thinking now of nothing in particular. As he approached, it opened automatically.

And when he had entered, it closed behind him.

XXXIII

MODYUN AWAKENED, and thought: I suppose suicide would be the simplest solution. But just plain making sure there are no children could be equally effective.

Whichever, and by whatever means, Man must end his line.

He yawned, stretched, and sat up on the bed in the little room which adjoined the control room of the lifeboat. The "day" lights had come on, which was, perhaps, why he had awakened. In the far back of his mind was a question, a puzzlement. It was too faint a feeling for him to take note of at this moment.

He climbed out of the bed—and almost fell over Roozb, who lay on the floor in a deep slumber. "Hey!" said Modyun.

Other figures, he saw quickly, were stretched out on the floor beyond Roozb. These stirred and sat up, and became recognizable in order of heads popping up as Dooldn, Narrl, and Ichdohz. The three animal-men scrambled to their feet, and all made a rush for Modyun, each in turn tripping over Roozb.

Narrl reached the human being first. "You all right, bub?" he asked.

Modyun was surprised. "Of course. How should I be?"

Dooldn, who had paused to give Roozb a shake, ceased his effort, and straightened. "I guess he's busy fighting his ancient hibernation instinct. Usually hits him during a certain period of each year—" His words obviously referred to the bear-man, but as he reached that point, he had a belated awareness of what Modyun had said. "How *should* you be?" he echoed. "Listen," he went on belligerently, "you said last night you'd indicate for an explanation in the morning of what happened. It's morning, fella."

"How do you mean?" The human being was astounded. "Explanation of what?"

He stopped. A lightning flash of memory stabbed through his mind. "I went through that door . . ." he mumbled.

"Yeah, and then what?" Ichdohz grunted the words.

Modyun glanced around the circle of questioning eyes. Even Roozb had sat up, and was gazing at him sleepily, He shook his head—he could feel his own eyes wide and dismayed. "I don't remember. How did I get here?"

The bear-man said, "You tell it, Narrl. You got a slick tongue."

"Nothing much to tell," said Narrl. "You went in; we saw you. Then somewhat more than an hour went by. Part of that time, the Earth army overran the place, climbed the steps, went into the building, also. Then we got an indication call from you to come and carry Soodleel, and we did. And then you said you had to go back to keep some promise, but since night was falling we persuaded you to stay until morning, and here we are."

"What'd I have to go back for?" Modyun was blank. "What kind of promise?"

"You didn't say."

Slowly, Modyun sank back onto the bed. "Sounds like spontaneous amnesia," he said slowly. "I'll have to be careful how I break through that."

Dooldn said in an awed voice, "You mean, hypnotism?"

The human being nodded soberly. "They must have got past my defenses." He could scarcely contain his amazement. "I'll be damned." He explained. "That's their method of control. A purpose is implanted, and then they've got you."

He was about to go on, when he remembered the thought that he had awakened with. He said, "Listen, I'm supposed to kill myself. No!" he corrected. "I have to make sure that Soodleel and I don't procreate. The human species has to end—"

Once more he came to a stop. He was like a man confronted by too many thoughts at one time. Sitting there on the edge of the bed, he fought to recover from confusion. "Soodleel!"—he picked up the name—"you say you carried her here. Where is she?"

The animal-men looked at each other significantly, and then shook their heads sorrowfully at each other. "Boy, this guy is really lost," said Dooldn.

Roozb said gently, "Modyun, look on the bed behind you."

Modyun turned slowly, not quite believing he could have been so unaware. He spent the first few seconds, then, analyzing that he had been lying slightly faced outward, and his initial impulse had been to get up. So his back had been toward Soodleel.

With that self-explanation satisfactorily out of the way, he

149

was able to look at the woman. The same golden hair . . . her face unchanged from when I first saw her . . . Even in sleep she radiated an intense—no other word for it—aliveness!

I wonder if I ever looked that energetic—It was the first time such a thought had ever crossed his mind. How did he appear to those who saw him?

Without glancing away from the woman, he asked, "What's wrong with her?"

"You told us she was unconscious. So we made a stretcher and carried her here." The speaker was Narrl. "And she hasn't changed since we brought her."

Modyun felt a great wonder. "I said all this last night, just as if I knew? Why didn't I bring her back to consciousness?"

It developed that he had been reluctant to interfere with the natural awakening, which apparently he had believed the previous evening would presently occur.

"I suppose," said Modyun in a baffled tone, "I must have known last night what I was doing. So I'd better not do anything hasty."

"*I* think," came the voice of Roozb, "we'd better hold a council of war, or something."

Something for sure, thought Modyun.

It was an hour later. They had eaten. They sat in the control room, a sober group. Modyun drew a deep breath.

"Here goes," he said, "I'm picturing me walking up to that door. Now, I'm going to indicate memory. I'll try to tell you fellows as I go what happens . . ."

XXXIV

As MODYUN entered, a Nunuli rose from behind a desk directly across from the door about twenty feet distant.

"Sign in here," he said.

He held in one hand what looked like a pen, and with the other pointed down at what appeared to be a guest book.

Modyun had stopped just inside the entrance. He consciously restrained his impulse to do at once what someone requested, and remained where he was, and glanced around. Not a large room, but high. The upcurving walls seemed to be made of the same gleaming whitish plastic as the walks and fences outside. There were two doors visible, other than the one through which he had come: one on either side of what, for want of a better term, he now thought of as a reception desk. The doors were huge—at least ten feet high—and ornately decorated with a gold leaf design. The entire place was as brightly lighted as the day outside by a method that Modyun did not attempt to analyze.

Satisfied with his swift examination, he walked slowly forward. Inside him, all perception receptors were switched on. He could feel the floor hard under his shoes, and the scraping of the cloth of the inside of his trousers on his legs and thighs. The shirt rubbed his chest and arms. The air felt warm, tingling in his lungs—the extra oxygen felt good. From his body came a dozen other proprioceptive sensations; and every message that came reported "all-well."

Presently, he was at the desk; and he looked down—at a blank page. As he studied it, he was aware from the corner of his eyes that the pen in the fingers of the Nunuli's outstretched hand was only inches from him.

He had two thoughts as he stood there. Both were critical of what was happening. The first thought: This was a setting that had been arranged for a person from Earth. The anteroom, the reception desk, the guest book—it was an incredibly simplified (no doubt hastily arranged) parallel to an old human institution:

the business office. He presumed that the familiar scene was intended to lull him. Perhaps they expected that he would automatically go through the motions which went with such a setting. The second thought grew out of the first. It was: Since they had taken this much trouble, then another scheme against him was now going forward.

In his brain, all indications were set to trigger. But fact was, he did not want to be involved on this lesser-than-Zouvg level. So he shook his head, as the animals did, meaning no.

"I have an appointment," he said.

The Nunuli did not argue his refusal. "This way, sir." He motioned toward the door to Modyun's left.

Modyun did not move. The other's words evoked from him not just one but a series of sensory awarenesses. The tone of voice. The way the Nunuli held his body as he spoke: a tiny puffing out of the muscles. And—most important—the emotion (a kind of slyness) that came to him from the "noise" in the being's brain.

Still another plot? What could it possibly be? First, the sense of wrongness in the signing of the guest book, now the same wrongness in the room he was to go into.

It cost Modyun a distinct effort to restrain himself from examining out of sheer curiosity what was beyond the left door. Later, he thought, I will go through that door, and I will sign the guest book.

He ought to know what they related to.

Aloud, he said, "Could I go into that room first?" He pointed to the door at his right.

"Of course." Courteously.

It sounded, felt, vibrated, resonated—correct.

The Nunuli walked over to the door, opened it, and held it. Approaching Modyun noted the immediate interior was a small alcove. The room itself was evidently off to the farther right. He could see nothing of it. As he came to the threshold, he did not pause, but stepped across and in.

Two things happened almost simultaneously: the door clicked shut behind him with a metallic sound, and ahead the lights went out.

In the abrupt darkness there in the Zouvg stronghold, he hesitated. But it was for a second only. Then he walked the ten feet of the alcove, turned to the left, and headed towards a chair, the presence of which he sensed by means of a composite of awareness. He walked fourteen paces to it, and sat down.

From the blackness, a voice said, "So you have allowed yourself to be trapped."

For bare instants after the words were spoken, Modyun's attention was held by the fact that the Zouvgite, like the Nunuli in the anteroom, also spoke the universal Earth language.

They've gone to a lot of trouble for one human being.

The awareness ran its course. And the sinister meaning of the words, by-passing the language in which they were enunciated—just like that—moved to the fore of his mind. Modyun continued to trust his original perception that this was the correct room for him to be in. As for what had been said, he considered the words and examined the environment in which they had been uttered.

He had already, at the instant of entering, sensed the body heat and presence of another living being. Just one person only, located about a dozen feet in front of the chair and slightly to his left. A faint alien odor permeated the room. He perceived that the being from whom it came was standing, and that he had spoken from a point at least a foot higher than Modyun at his tallest.

Was the committee member on a dais? It didn't feel like it to Modyun's pervasive awareness. He accordingly concluded that the Zouvg was a nine or nine and a half foot giant.

Interesting—hey!

Having now sensed that the committee member was staring at him from the pitch blackness, as if some kind of vision was involved, Modyun turned his attention to what had been said.

Have I been a victim of the instant persuasion from which the Zouvg derive their overlord power?

As Modyun recalled it, the other's voice had had a different texture than any he had ever heard. And of course there was the sensational directness of statement in the meaning—*trapped!*

His tense self-examination ended. Nothing wrong yet . . . I'm still untouched.

He was able, with that thought, to become aware of another emotion: disappointment. Already, the meeting with the committee member was not as he had somehow visualized it: an open, face-to-face dialogue. The speed of the opening moves, and the frame—the darkness—had already (he had to admit it) had

153

a telescoping effect. In such a confrontation, one started, not at the beginning, but at some peak of intensity.

Modyun did a little telescoping himself. "I am unhappily realizing," he said, "that your words and manner imply that you are not intending to abandon your conquest of the galaxy."

The first reply of the Zouvg was that he walked closer and presently stood in the near darkness looking down at the man in the chair. The second reply was: "We seem to be having a misunderstanding. We have no plans for conquest. Where did you get an idea like that?"

Modyun sat back, belatedly now remembering that the same words had been spoken by the ship's Nunuli Master. At the time he had visualized the consequences of what that servant-people was doing: busily taking over planets on behalf of the Zouvgs. On Earth, the humans gone. Gunya remorselessly attacked.

He found his voice abruptly and pointed out these hard facts, concluding, "I have the impression that variations of these methods have been applied to tens of thousands of other planets."

"What we do is not conquest," said the Zouvg. "We are simply and firmly cancelling out accidental evolutionary developments of wrong-life forms. As soon as the correct evolutionary line is established on a planet, we allow it to proceed for a while, with guidance, but finally without additional interference. By no stretch of the imagination can that be considered conquest."

Dazzled, Modyun parted his lips. Then he closed them. In a spate of sentences, he had been given—*the explanation*.

For God's sake, he thought. An attack on those fittest everywhere who survived the evolutionary gauntlet on their planet.

It was an amazing concept.

Not even when man was modifying the animals was *that* idea at issue. And later, when, spurred by the Nunuli, human beings modified themselves, it was merely to emphasize a trait that had already surfaced in the muddy stream of natural selection.

"By what and whose, standard," he asked, "is a selection of the proper racial strain made?"

"On every planet," said the Zouvgite, "we developed the naturally longest-lived life-form. Can you think of a better standard than longevity?"

The voice ceased. Modyun waited politely for the being to enlarge upon the meaning. When several seconds had gone by, he detected in the evenness of the other's breathing that no additional explanation was intended.

"Look . . ." he began vaguely. He stopped, sat there for several more seconds, and then asked: "You are a long-lived race—is that not so?"

"Long-lived is an incorrect way of describing what we have. We are immortal." The voice was proud. "It is one of our two most important qualities."

Modyun presumed silently that the other important quality was the Zouvgite ability to control minds. But he decided not to be distracted by that.

What he said was, "In short, you have chosen as significant a quality which your race apparently acquired by natural unmodified selection. I say 'apparently' because it's a point I want to bring up again."

The committee member was calm. "We were completely objective. We evaluated *all* the desirable traits in hundreds of races—"

"And finally decided that your own was best," Modyun flashed, "without inquiring as to how it came about."

"I repeat"—was there just a touch of irritation in the tone?— "can you think of a better trait than longevity?"

"Yes," said Modyun, "the human indication system. Yes. The human live-and-let-live philosophy. You see," he broke off, "I think of human traits, and you think of Zouvg. Very subjective, both of us, aren't we?"

"What your words tell me," was the cold reply, "is that since we have you here completely under our control, further conversation is a waste of time."

So they were back to that.

Modyun sat very still in his chair, perceiving. And as far as he could determine, nothing had changed. In all these minutes— beginning to be a respectable total—there had been no stirring in his indication system. So whatever they were doing, it was more basic than *that*. Both the Ylem and space were silent in their energy-control frequences. The entire near universe moved within its frame of atomic and molecular logic, undisturbed by interfering minds—which suggested the problem was inside him, not outside.

As he uneasily considered *those* possibilities, it occurred to Modyun that the time had come for whatever it was he intended to do here. What, he wasn't sure.

155

I came to have a conversation. I am having it. It is going nowhere . . .

Not feeling sure of where he was going either, he began tentatively, "Biology is a subject which, as a result if our improvement by the Nunuli, we came to understand perhaps better than anyone."

There was a sound from the darkness. It came from the huge being standing there in front of him. Not words, but a voice noise. Derisive laughter?

The Zouvgite spoke in a tolerant tone. "Basically, we don't have to take any action now. Control of you was established long ago. You must know that no one can do anything against the way he *is*. The individual may even observe the nature of the battle he *should* fight—which is the stage you seem to have arrived at—but you are forever bound by the fact that your skin can be punctured, your heart can stop, groups of cells in your brain have specific abilities—and no other. For example, despite your indication system, you human beings have achieved a life span of less than two thousand Earth years. Even that you owe to the Nunuli improvement of human being."

"True," acknowledged the Man. "However, I've been intending to analyze that for you, and—"

The Zouvgite cut him off.

"In order to show you how positive we feel, we challenge you to use your indication system against us. You will find you cannot."

"You are asking the impossible," Modyun protested. "The word 'against' is not a meaningful term in my mind. I am not against you."

"Exactly," said the Zouvgite with satisfaction, "as our servant race programmed you to be."

"It would be immensely difficult for me deliberately to take a destructive action against anyone," said the Man.

"Precisely," said the committee member, happily. "This is your frame. As I've said, you're battling vaguely against that forever condition, but essentially you can do no other than you have— being the way you are."

"Hmmm," said Modyun. "I can see we don't entirely understand each other." He thereupon repeated a remark he had once heard Roozb make, to Dooldn's great disgust. "There's more than one way to skin a cat," he said.

156

"I don't understand that," said the Zouvgite.

Modyun did not reply.

He couldn't. He was back in the lifeboat, blank of memory.

"And that's the end of that sequence," he said in disgust."

"But what cat did you intend to skin by what method?" asked Roozb, with a sly glance at a red-faced Dooldn.

"I'm sorry I used that comparison," said Modyun, who was sitting across the commissary table from the jaguar-man. "My apologies, Dooldn."

"It's okay," muttered the big cat-man. "I'm more scared than mad. So that's a Zouvgite. Boy!"

Ichdohz was shaking his head. "Fellows," he said, "we've got a pansy here." He scowled at Modyun. "He's not frightened, but he sure doesn't know how to fight."

"I was about to start," protested Modyun.

"Then you're talking phony. You told that Zouvgite you couldn't do anything. Now you tell us you can."

They were all staring at the Man accusingly.

"Yeah, what is this hypocrisy?" asked Narrl.

Roozb said, "One thing we always figured you for was honesty. And now you gave him all that doubletalk. Don't get me wrong," the bear-man finished hastily. "We've got to beat those SOBs somehow."

"I was going to attack them through the Ylem," Modyun explained, "and by the only fair method open to me. Listen . . ."

When Modyun had completed his explanation, Dooldn said blankly, "and you figure that's what you must have done?"

"Yes."

"But the moment you did it, that was the end of your memory for that sequence."

Modyun had to admit that certainly was what had happened. "I guess they must have counterattacked with another purpose."

Narrl chimed in. "This Ylem energy, would it have killed that lineup of Zouvgites?"

Modyun was shocked. "Of course not. That would be murder."

Dooldn threw up his hands. "Listen to this so-and-so!" he roared. He controlled himself with an effort and said, "Can you locate another bunch of energy like that in the Ylem?"

Modyun shook his head. "They're probably there. But that's

157

the only one I knew of. You've got to remember the Ylem is as big as space, except it has no time."

"What you're saying is, you've used up what you know about?" the jaguar-man persisted.

"That's what I intended to do," agreed Modyun defensively.

Dooldn's face was brick-red as he leaned back in his chair. "I'd better not say any more," he mumbled. "The biggest opportunity in the history of the galaxy muffled by a soft-hearted—" He seemed overcome, and finished in a choked voice, "Fellows, you take over!"

It was Roozb who spoke—diplomatically, "Okay, Modyun, why don't you indicate? We might as well find out what did happen."

XXXV

HE DID his test. Did it realistically. Assumed that he wouldn't have a second chance, and made the sample run the complete experiment. Like a general with a creative new idea for fighting a battle, he tried it out not in preliminary maneuvers but on the field.

Obviously, he couldn't attack a thousand high-powered brains set against his in the one-way lineup common to a situation where more than one hypnotist joined together to overwhelm the subject. So he made no direct approach. Instead, he used his indication awareness to search the Ylem for an already existent energy source, according to the unvarying laws involved.

Since the process was virtually instantaneous, he was not surprised when the silence in that night-enveloped room was broken by the Zouvg saying: "According to our instruments, you indicated. Yet nothing happened."

The Zouvg continued in the same irritated tone, "We all felt minor physical sensations on the Ylem level. But everybody knows that nothing can be initiated in the Ylem without preliminary planning. Naturally, these require no time in the Ylem itself, but there is a passage of time in our space world. And you haven't had that much time."

So they felt something. So he might as well recognize that discovery was inevitable.

He said with just a hint of his old courtesy, "What is now progressively happening is of course physiologic. As it gets stronger, don't be alarmed. But it must be faced that when a reversal is set right there is an actual shifting in the chemical bonds. This creates a peculiar . . ."

He paused, unhappily conscious of a sudden tension in the room. It was if the committee member was doing the Zouvg equivalent of perspiring nervously. Out of the blackness, the creature's voice came grimly, "Are you saying that you have physically manipulated me—us—in some way?"

159

"All I did," acknowledged Modyun courteously, "was to utilize the energy you originally put in the Ylem; utilize it as a carrier for a biologic readjustment indication. And it affected all those aligned with you, which you said was everybody. Now—"

"*What* original energy?"

"The explosion in the Ylem," said Modyun, "by which you destroyed the human beings behind the barrier. Where did you learn about the Ylem?"

"From a race now extinct." The Zouvgite spoke reluctantly.

"Another wrong evolutionary development, I suppose," said Modyun. "Well, I've got to tell you that their knowledge of the Ylem was not sophisticated. So that I was able to use the reaction energy from the explosion—which you will have to agree subsumes in its total force any combination of life energies—"

"And what"—the being interrupted harshly—"has this energy achieved?"

Modyun drew a deep breath. "The Zouvg race will now go properly forward on its correct evolutionary line. For the next few thousand years, the life span of the individual will be—I would guess—oh, seventy to eighty Earth years."

He had been progressively aware as he talked of a tense emotion building up in the being who towered above him in that night-black room. Suddenly—

"This reversal in us, which you have rectified," said the Zouvgite in a strained voice. "One of my associates has just asked me if the rectification can be nullified, and the original reversal restored?"

Modyun hesitated. He was startled by the speed of the reaction. Such an immense defeat he had inflicted on these people—yet here was virtually instant recovery.

Counterattack coming, he thought, tensely. He had taken the advantage open to him of their one unawareness. That was now done, and he had nothing else. What remained was *his* programming, which *they* understood.

Naturally, he had to reply honestly to their question. "I really hadn't thought about, but I perceive that the answer is yes. It would have to be done one at a time, which could be very tedious. But I must tell you that I have no intention of—"

Again, the response was at a mind-staggering speed, considering how enormous their state of shock must be. "We were the

160

only immortal race in the universe," said the Zouvgite, "and you have made us mortal. That's *wrong*."

In a way that was true. Anything unique like that, however arrived at, should probably not be interfered with. But they interfered with so many, Modyun argued with himself, that their argument seemed irrelevant.

I'm being attacked all right. I'm agreeing.

The Zouvgite urged, "There's nothing sacred about natural selection. On Earth you human beings interfered with it when you modified the animals—"

The voice said more. But for a little while that was all that Modyun heard. He had become physically unsteady. His vision blurred. Sound was a mumble inside his head. In a distant corner of his mind, he observed the perpetual distortion; and he thought in mild amazement: I am being controlled right now by those words.

Was it possible he was going to have to take the great risk of indicating to protect himself?

As he had that uneasy thought, he noticed that the disturbance seemed to be lessening. Was no more than a kind of vertigo; not really deadly; not even unbearable. It occurred to him that the abuse and mistreatment and conspiracies of these people had twisted the purity of his response. I've come a long way, he thought, probably most of it in the wrong direction. But under the circumstances he was not sorry.

He was so far recovered by the time he came to that realization, he was again aware of the committee member's voice.

". . . My colleague," the Zouvgite was saying, "proposes that we return the human female to you in return for restoring us. As he reasons it, you need this woman for the survival of your own species. She is unconscious and in danger. So he feels you have no alternative."

He felt stunned by the instant perfection of their logic. They had missed a fateful flaw in their own makeup. But, then, so had mankind. Already, the Zouvgites were recovering. It was not so certain that Man would, unless—

They've got me, he thought. I can't use my indication to force the information, because they can nullify that. But now they won't dare actually to do anything against me, since I'm the only one who can help them . . .

A perfect balance of power between Man and his most

dangerous opponent. The symmetry of it had a kind of sinister beauty.

Of course, there was still a problem.

"I'm willing to restore you. But I don't know how it can be arranged. You see"—he spread his hands, as Narrl often did—"the moment I return even one committee member to his former state, he's free. After that, no agreement can bind him to protect Soodleel."

He broke off, pensively, "I am accepting that she is in your possession. She admitted she was trapped. I picture her, with her nonviolent philosophy and passive womanly attitudes, being exceedingly trusting."

"That's it exactly," interrupted the Zouvg eagerly. "We were able to render her body unconscious, but naturally we were reluctant to make a direct attack on the indication system. But now there is in fact a reason for a quick decision on your part. Because we recognize the urgency, and also rather than waste any time, we find ourselves accepting that a person with your, uh, pure philosophy—however misguided it may be—would keep a promise once made. So"—with a rush—"if you will promise to restore us to our original condition during the next week, or sooner, we will tell you exactly where Soodleel is."

So I am under control. It seemed the only plausible interpretation.

He felt no different. He felt as if he could make a free decision . . . *I can promise, and then I can break my promise . . .* That was the way it felt inside.

But they were acting as if he wouldn't.

The Zouvgite said urgently, "You'd better decide. It's important for the woman's safety."

The decision was no longer a problem in any way. Modyun said simply, "Very well, I promise. Where is she?"

"She's in the room through that left door in the anteroom outside," blurted the other. "We had it rigged so that if you went in there you'd see her. During the moment of mental absorption with her condition, all thousand of us would make our attack on you."

Modyun's eyes widened. "Hmm," he said, "I wonder if that would have worked."

While he considered that, he had another thought. "This thousand business," he said. "How did you Zouvgites get yourselves down to that low a number?"

162

"It's one family," explained the committee member. His attention seemed to be elsewhere. "Obviously, where there are many families, one must eventually exterminate the others. That happened long ago—"

XXXVI

In the lifeboat, Modyun stood up. "That's when the animal soldiers came. The Nunuli and the Zouvg beat it into some passageway leading into the interior of the mountain. And I hurried out of the anteroom and took up a guard position in front of that left door. Some of the soldiers wanted to break the door down, but I just indicated them away one at a time.

He grew thoughtful. "They were actually a very peaceful lot. I can imagine, however, that they looked wild to the committee members, who had never allowed anyone behind their barrier and had no defense against a vast number of people. Whatever problem there might have been ended when I ordered the commissaries down. They were as hungry as they had ever been in their pampered lives, but they formed lines and took their turn like well-behaved citizens. As soon as I saw that, I called you guys, and you came with a stretcher for Soodleel."

Roozb said triumphantly, "I want you to notice that this time your memory ran all the way to the end. So they didn't get to you with their high-powered hypnotism."

"I noticed it," said Modyun.

He walked to the control board, and—aware that they were all watching him—pressed the button that opened the airlock. "I'd better be on my way," he said. He headed for the double door, paused just inside the entranceway, and said, "I'll be back tomorrow morning. So just wait here, will you?"

Having spoken, he strode outside, and started to climb the slope that would presently bring him to the garden and the Zouvgite building half a mile away. He had proceeded about two hundred feet, when he became aware that the four animal-men had emerged from the lifeboat, and were running in the same direction as he. Modyun continued on his way, since they did not call out to him; but he was not surprised when they fell in step beside him, breathing hard.

"Where you going?" Narrl said, gasping.

Modyun stopped. He explained about his promise to the Zouv-gites. "So you see, that's what I've got to go and do." He was about to resume his walking, when he saw an odd expression on Dooldn's face.

The jaguar-man said in a strangled tone, "You've got to be kidding!"

"How do you mean?" Puzzled.

"You're not going to keep a promise like that to the biggest SOBs that ever lived?"

"A promise is a promise," said Modyun. And then he said, startled, "Hey!"

They had grabbed him.

"You're not going nowhere," growled Roozb.

They were leading him back toward the lifeboat before Modyun clearly realized their intent. "Look, fellows," he warned then, "I'll have to use my indication on you if you don't stop."

"Okay," defied Dooldn, "if you can do that to us, your only pals, you just go ahead, bub."

"But my promise—" began Modyun vaguely.

Dooldn cut him off. "Remember you once asking me what my work was before this expedition? And I wouldn't tell."

Modyun remembered. But it seemed an irrelevant recollection. "So?" he said.

"Well," said Dooldn, "I was a guard in a hospital for the insane." That was all he said.

The four animal-men continued to hold Modyun firmly. They walked him along, pushing at his resisting body, unheeding of his protests, daring him, in effect, to overwhelm them with his indication system—and that was the one thing he couldn't bring himself to do. Straight to the control chair and into it; and held him there while he reluctantly manipulated the instruments that presently started them back toward the big ship, which waited in an orbit over 23,000 miles up.

It was as he completed that action that he sensed an indication stirring . . . A superspeed part of his brain recognized the trigger-ing sensation as comparatively harmless.

I'm going to have a fantasy . . .

They're doing this. They're desperate as they see me leaving. Should I put up a counterindication that will react in case I'm threatened, but see what the fantasy is?

Yes.

At once, an hallucinatory scene: he was back in the anteroom of the Zouvgite building. He had the pen in his right hand, and he was bending over the guest book. Somehow, he understood the meaning of what had happened. The indication that had been stirred in his brain would, in effect, sign for him as if he were right there.

All right.

In the fantasy, he actually seemed to sign, and even started to straighten up when—

Modyun awakened in darkness, remembering what Dooldn had said, and realized: I'll be damned. My animal friends handled me like an insane person.

What bothered him was that he could see a relevance. *I was.*

I was programmed and am a product of race improvement. And he had never until recently used his intelligence to transcend that. If that wasn't insanity, what was?

He lay there in the quiet darkness; and now that his eyes were accustoming, he saw that he was in his cabin aboard the big earth ship. Vaguely, he could make out the shapes of two people sitting in chairs beside the bed. Presently, he was even able to evaluate that the two were Roozb and Dooldn. They're watching over me. They're my friends. He felt a warm, sad feeling about that. Sad, because he suspected they would feel badly when the last man and woman did what had to be done: removed themselves from among the living.

He suspected that idea had been triggered in him from Man's long-ago programming by the Nunuli. But, he realized, the origin of a truth made no difference.

Inside every human male was a secret, slithery, bloated, infinitely stubborn, mindless, mental-emotional *thing* that made him the most detestable of all creatures of the galaxy.

In the old days, given the slightest opening, he had taken full advantage of *any* chance opportunity to raise himself at the expense of other human beings. No political system could contain him. And there was no limit to his greed.

The Zouvgites are right. The human race must cease.

It occurred to him, belatedly, that they had probably planted their purpose during the peculiar dizziness he had experienced. The feeling he had had then of easily recovering was false. A neat illusion, performed by experts.

166

Still, it had been quite a battle. They knocked me out, then I knocked them out. Now, they've triggered their knockout of me as a revenge, or pressure.

Boy, he thought.

Both races were unfit. But, of course, what the Zouvgites did with themselves was none of his business. So he would have to undo what he had done to them. Obviously.

From the near darkness, Roozb's voice came, "Dooldn, I think this guy's awake."

"Huh!" The jaguar-man seemed confused for a few moments. Then he came awkwardly to his feet.

He's going to turn on the light . . . Modyun braced himself involuntarily. Yet, as the light came on, he blinked, and squeezed his eyes.

"Yeah, he's awake all right." That was Dooldn. Both animal-men stepped towards the bed and bent over him.

Roozb said grimly, "We've been perceiving your thoughts. Soodleel indicated a connection for us before she went off to the dance. And, boy, are you a lost soul."

"How do you mean, lost?" Modyun spoke automatically. "What dance?"

The bear-man ignored his questions. "She says—Soodleel— that you're going to have to indicate away that hypnotism yourself. It would be an invasion of privacy for her to do it."

"True," agreed Modyun. His mind poised. "B-but what about her connecting you with me, thought-wise? That's invasion."

"She figured that was our business," explained Dooldn with satisfaction. "And, brother, we don't have any such scruples. Ready, Roozb?"

"Ready," said the bear-man, tensely.

"Listen, bub," said Dooldn, "you're going to have to make a decision. Either kill us—that's the way Soodleel set it up, at our request—or indicate that Zouvgite hypnotism out of your system. Get ready for the beating of your life."

Modyun sat up in the bed, and looked hastily from one determined face to the other. Startled by what he saw there, he said, "I'll have to indicate against you—"

"That's what'll kill us," said Roozb, "the way Soodleel set it up."

Without pause, he launched his big fist at Modyun's chest. The blow was so hard, it took the man's breath away. "For God's

167

sake—" he gasped. He was unable to finish. At that instant, Dooldn's fist struck him a terrific blow on the side of the head. "Indicate away that hypnotism!" the jaguar-man snarled.

"Look," Modyun yelled, "it would be unfair—" Roozb's fist hit his jaw squarely, and he made a glub sound. "It's wrong," Modyun mumbled. "Their immortality—" Dooldn stopped those words with a belting blow to the stomach. "Indicate, you so-and-so!"

Somewhere, Modyun began to fight back. Later, he was amazed to discover that he was on his knees near the door, and that Roozb was choking him, and bellowing, "Indicate, you bastard!"

The fact is, Modyun thought finally, somewhat vaguely, suggestion can take many forms. This method is very convincing.

About a minute after, he was lying on the floor with Dooldn astride his legs, and Roozb with knees on his biceps. The bear-man's fist was lifted, and his intent seemed to be to smash Modyun in the face with it.

It was too much. The Man cringed. "Don't hit me!" he said. "I'll do it."

In a corner of his mind was a greater wonder. His thought was that the Zouvgites had surely never taken into account that someone would care what happened to human beings.

Above him, the poised fist relaxed. "Okay, indicate."

Modyun did so, and then he sighed, "It's still wrong, but it's done."

They pulled him to his feet. They embraced him. Roozb was almost in tears. "Boy," he choked, "That's the toughest thing I ever did. But now"—he broke off—"we've got one more job for you to do. Four billion human beings decided life wasn't worth living—right?"

Modyun waited. He had a feeling no answer was necessary. And, in fact, the bear-man continued, "So you've probably got that kind of thinking going on inside you without any Zouvgite hypnotism needed to help it along. Right?"

It was right, all right.

"So," said the bear-man, "It's up to your pals to make sure that doesn't happen. Now, listen. You're going to get that female pregnant in the next couple of weeks, and we're just the guys that are going to stay right here and see that it gets done; or you get a worse beating than this one."

"Well-l-ll," said Modyun doubtfully. "I suppose it's all right. After all, she *is* my wife."

He was laughing and doing a jig. All around him, the animal people were dancing with abandon. But he was the most free of all. He had had at all times only conscious restraints on his motor centers, and those were now gone for some time. The rhythmic music flowed through his ears, and stimulated the entire motion area. The effect was a fast but remarkably graceful dance.

Skilfully, he guided himself through the vast throng until, as he took one more spin, he came face to face with the woman, grabbing at her at the exact moment that she, laughing also, spun towards him.

As they came together, she quite happily and laughingly accepted his arms around her, and put her hands up to fit in with the movement.

It was as she completed the connecting step that she, for the first time, looked up into his face.

XXXVII

ONCE MORE, the thought—or rather, a variant of it—passed through Modyun's mind: *All this is very convincing.*

He noticed the idea as it flitted by, a single set, one solitary observation of the self finally being aware.

In that instant of time, he had his awful realization: *Not convincing enough.*

Below him, the woman's face wavered a little. The two of them continued their dance. But the illusion—which was what Modyun now perceived it to be—held reasonably steady.

Yet he was no longer a part of it. He waited, curious, for his true perceptions to surface. And was not particularly surprised when the next manifestation was not reality but another hallucination: of all people, Bunlt, the rat-man, and he were suddenly standing facing each other. And Bunlt was saying uncertainly, "My . . . philosophy? What's a philosophy?"

They stood, the two of them, the tall, powerful human, and the tall, somewhat thinner rat-man . . . stood there in that glittering marble hallway of the courtroom building back on Earth, as Modyun explained that a philosophy was a permanent *reason.* So—

"What was your reason for stealing that car?"

"I told you, I figured I've got just as much right." Bunlt paused, looked helpless, spread his hands, waited.

"What you're really saying, then," said Modyun, "is that in this world created by humans, the hyena-men can take over legal control of a planet while the rest of the people get involved in a squabble over a tiny violation of equality which they happen to notice next door?"

The rat-man blinked. "Hey," he said, "is that what I said?" He seemed impressed.

As Bunlt completed his words, his image and the court hallway faded out like a scene on a film going bland.

Yet, though Modyun could see nothing, his feet were on solid hardness. He was patient with the condition, convinced that his brain was still trying to surface, obviously against opposition. The tiny dialogue between Bunlt and himself, which had never taken place in real life, was another effort on the part of the Zouvgites to invalidate humankind. They had shown him once more that man and his intelligent animals were incorrigibly spoiled brats—and irrational.

Actually, thought Modyun, the human condition was much worse than Bunlt's little demonstration. Behind the trivial resistance to someone else's aggrandizement there waited in every man an egotistic insanity.

A vaulting impulse crouched, tirelessly seeking a pathway through the barriers of other people's resisting, competing purposes. If that tangle of programmed, brain-washed opposition ever for an instant opened a way, as it sometimes accidentally did, if suddenly for an instant the pathway was visible, the waiting madman darted into it, and along it. *Whatever* it led to—kingship, money, property, control of labor—by whatever means—murder, torture, or imprisonment of *all* opponents without mercy—he took it; he did it.

And the human woman was willing to be right there beside her god—an unthinking princess, never asking how the man had achieved; requiring only that he be up there at the apex . . . and do what was necessary to stay there.

Those men and women who didn't make it waited, frustrated and impatient, for *their* opportunity.

The Zouvgites are right. The human race is not fit to survive . . .

Modyun was not surprised that the realization didn't seem to bother him. He had become progressively aware of a change in himself.

All this fighting. So sustained. They had been remorselessly determined; and thus they had forced upon him by one action after the other, a new programming. Beginning with his body's automatic defense indication against that first hyena-man . . . on through the colossal battle (which he had not recognized as such) against the mighty singularity attack, and now finally this savage assault on him as an individual . . .

The stupid idiots, Modyun thought, they have turned me into a warrior without my noticing.

As he had that thought, his perception . . . cleared.

He was, he saw, standing in front of the transparent doors of

171

the Zouvg building. Around him, behind him, was a great silence.

Of course—he thought—what else?

It was the original moment of his arrival.

The Zouvgites had made their collective effort to control his mind in these very first moments of his coming here. And all these deadly seconds his brain and its abilities, so magnificently perfected by the Nunuli, had fought its silent battle for survival on that level of reality below consciousness where, alas, Man actually operated—

Endlessness and foreverness of internal, underlying mental forces that had brought humankind to the brink, with never a single questioning, always an accepting mindlessness of momentary moods and attitudes, to the point where one man and one woman now stood alone against eternity.

Once more, Modyun looked around at the mountain scenery, and then back to the doors, and then inwardly upon himself; and there was no doubt. "This," he felt, "is real. This time I'm here."

There remained only his own decision about his own future.

Deliberately, Modyun opened the door, and walked inside the anteroom. The Nunuli Master, who waited behind the desk twenty feet away, held out the pen and pointed at the guest book.

Modyun accepted the pen and bending, signed firmly and without hesitation. What he wrote was:

"Modyun, human being of Earth, here to negotiate a permanent peace on the basis of a victor in battle dictating to a defeated enemy—"

Only when he had written the words did he notice that they were, in effect, a complete denial of his lifetime philosophy. Boy, he thought, once you get a change in inner feeling, it really is different.

What he felt, signalled that a race did what it must to survive. Had no negative thoughts about group existence. Within such a frame, dissenting individuals might anticipate that growth and change would eventually eliminate the unpleasant traits of evolutionary adjustment to a specific environment. But the species *never* agreed to such a qualifying limitation.

A race accepted life.

Yes, it was a different feeling. Yes, yes, yes, yes.

After a moment's longer consideration, Modyun used the pen once more, adding to what he had written the words: "—on the basis of live and let live, really."

172

He underlined the key thought. *"Really."*

And then he straightened to his full height, realizing as he did so that he was experiencing an emotion he had never had before, a kind of glee, because the act of signing had produced no repercussions.

"Which door?" Modyun asked, and his voice was a crashing sound into the silence of that anteroom.

There was a long pause. A strange, tense, startled expression was on that smooth, gray face. He's getting instructions, thought Modyun.

Slowly, reluctantly, the Nunuli arm came up, and pointed at the door to the right.

The victorious fighter's glee accompanied Modyun into the room beyond the door.

THE SILKIE
by A. E. van Vogt

THE SILKIE – a living spaceship impervious to heat and cold, virtually indestructible, and capable of travelling at supersonic speeds – similar to a human being, but not the same. Highly intelligent. The Silkie – able to live under the oceans with the ease of a dolphin and the speed of a shark. The Silkie – a modern angel or a computerised demon? The Silkie – friend of Earth, or a pitiless, alien destroyer? Once again A. E. van Vogt demonstrates his mastery of the science fiction genre in the incredible adventures of THE SILKIE.

On sale at newsagents and booksellers everywhere.

NEW ENGLISH LIBRARY

NEL BESTSELLERS

T046 133	HOW GREEN WAS MY VALLEY	*Richard Llewellyn*	£1.00
T039 560	I BOUGHT A MOUNTAIN	*Thomas Firbank*	95p
T033 988	IN THE TEETH OF THE EVIDENCE	*Dorothy L. Sayers*	90p
T038 149	THE CARPETBAGGERS	*Harold Robbins*	£1.50
T040 917	TO SIR WITH LOVE	*E.R. Braithwaite*	75p
T041 719	HOW TO LIVE WITH A NEUROTIC DOG	*Stephen Baker*	75p
T040 925	THE PRIZE	*Irving Wallace*	£1.65
T034 755	THE CITADEL	*A.J. Cronin*	£1.10
T042 189	STRANGER IN A STRANGE LAND	*Robert Heinlein*	£1.25
T037 053	79 PARK AVENUE	*Harold Robbins*	£1.25
T042 308	DUNE	*Frank Herbert*	£1.50
T045 137	THE MOON IS A HARSH MISTRESS	*Robert Heinlein*	£1.25
T040 933	THE SEVEN MINUTES	*Irving Wallace*	£1.50
T038 130	THE INHERITORS	*Harold Robbins*	£1.25
T035 689	RICH MAN, POOR MAN	*Irwin Shaw*	£1.50
T037 134	EDGE 27: DEATH DRIVE	*George G. Gilman*	75p
T037 541	DEVIL'S GUARD	*Robert Elford*	£1.25
T042 774	THE RATS	*James Herbert*	80p
T042 340	CARRIE	*Stephen King*	80p
T042 782	THE FOG	*James Herbert*	90p
T033 740	THE MIXED BLESSING	*Helen Van Slyke*	£1.25
T037 061	BLOOD AND MONEY	*Thomas Thompson*	£1.50
T038 629	THIN AIR	*Simpson & Burger*	95p
T038 602	THE APOCALYPSE	*Jeffrey Konvitz*	95p

NEL P.O. BOX 11, FALMOUTH TR10 9EN, CORNWALL.

Postage charge:

U.K. Customers. Please allow 25p for the first book plus 10p per copy for each additional book ordered to a maximum charge of £1.05 to cover the cost of postage and packing, in addition to cover price.

B.F.P.O. & Eire. Please allow 25p for the first book plus 10p per copy for the next 8 books, thereafter 5p per book, in addition to cover price.

Overseas Customers. Please allow 40p for the first book plus 12p per copy for each additional book, in addition to cover price.

Please send cheque or postal order (no currency).

Name ....

Address ....

....

Title ....

While every effort is made to keep prices steady, it is sometimes necessary to increase prices at short notice. New English Library reserve the right to show on covers and charge new retail prices which may differ from those advertised in the text or elsewhere.